MW00476210

# KILLED WITH A KISS

# KILLED WITH A KISS

*(A Lacey Doyle Cozy Mystery-Book 5)*

FIONA GRACE

Copyright © 2020 by Fiona Grace. All rights reserved. Except as permitted under the U.S. Copyright Act of 1976, no part of this publication may be reproduced, distributed or transmitted in any form or by any means, or stored in a database or retrieval system, without the prior permission of the author. This ebook is licensed for your personal enjoyment only. This ebook may not be re-sold or given away to other people. If you would like to share this book with another person, please purchase an additional copy for each recipient. If you're reading this book and did not purchase it, or it was not purchased for your use only, then please return it and purchase your own copy. Thank you for respecting the hard work of this author. This is a work of fiction. Names, characters, businesses, organizations, places, events, and incidents either are the product of the author's imagination or are used fictionally. Any resemblance to actual persons, living or dead, is entirely coincidental. Jacket image Copyright Helen Hotson, used under license from Shutterstock.com.

# FIONA GRACE

Debut author Fiona Grace is author of the LACEY DOYLE COZY MYSTERY series, comprising nine books (and counting); of the TUSCAN VINEYARD COZY MYSTERY series, comprising three books (and counting); of the DUBIOUS WITCH COZY MYSTERY series, comprising three books (and counting); and of the BEACHFRONT BAKERY COZY MYSTERY series, comprising three books (and counting).

MURDER IN THE MANOR (A Lacey Doyle Cozy Mystery—Book 1) is available as a free download on Amazon!

Fiona would love to hear from you, so please visit www.fionagrace-author.com to receive free ebooks, hear the latest news, and stay in touch.

# TABLE OF CONTENTS

# CHAPTER ONE

L acey hung the final picture frame on the wall in the low-ceilinged corridor of her cottage and stepped back to admire her handiwork.

"There!" she said, proud of her most recent DIY accomplishment.

Chester, her English shepherd, was sitting patiently beside her. He barked.

"Thanks," Lacey said, smiling at him. "It *does* look great, doesn't it?"

Lacey had recently invested in several antique paintings to decorate her home with. She'd been inspired by the home decor of an elderly antiques collector she'd met on vacation, whose beautifully decorated home made her realize just how woefully lacking in the personal touch her own cottage was. She'd also come into some money after selling a rare Roman-era gold coin (for an eye-wateringly high sum she was almost embarrassed to admit). After putting half the money in a college fund for her nephew, Frankie, paying off a chunk of the mortgage, and buying a thank-you gift for her friend Gina (a fancy hydroponic system for her greenhouse), she'd promptly set about splurging for her home. Her first purchase had been a hallway runner, a genuine antique Indian Amritsar in earthy red and terracotta colors that had once adorned the corridor of a New Delhi hotel. Then she'd set about sourcing some artwork for the walls—a nineteenth-century John William Gilroy oil painting of a fishing boat on the coast, a gorgeous depiction of azaleas by Francis B. Savage, and a Harry Williams landscape dated 1860. There was still a large empty space beside the big window on the second-floor landing, but Crag Cottage was finally starting to look like her own.

Lacey was surprised by just how different it looked from her old apartment in New York City. In her prior life as an interior design assistant, she'd adopted a minimalist, sleek, contemporary style, so it had come as something of a shock to her to realize her actual, personal, unfettered taste was this hodge-podge of chintz and patterns and bright paintings, in a higgledy-piggledy old cottage by the sea.

"I think that's enough for one day," Lacey said to Chester. "I can't wait to show Tom."

Her boyfriend was coming over later that evening for a well overdue date, and Lacey was very much looking forward to showing off all the changes she'd made to the cottage's decor. The summer had been incredibly hectic for them both workwise. Tom's patisserie and Lacey's antiques store were both located on the busy High Street of Wilfordshire, England, where the footfall seemed to increase exponentially in tandem with the sunshine. Added to their busyness, their one chance at a getaway over a long weekend hadn't exactly panned out the way she'd hoped. Though Studdleton Bay had offered Lacey all the charms of the British seaside she loved, her family tagging along, and a murder during their visit, had put a damper on anything romantic.

Chester trotted behind Lacey into the kitchen, his claws making a soft clickety-click on the tiles. Here, too, Lacey's newfound enthusiasm to personalize her cottage was on glorious display. Inspired by the old appraiser's crockery collection, Lacey had decided to begin collecting teacups. There was nothing more representative of her new English life than a cup of tea, after all, and Tom had a collection of teapots, so they matched. So far, she'd amassed a grand total of three cups: an iconic Wedgwood Renaissance style cup in cream with gold trimming and matching saucer, a fuchsia rose patterned Queen Anne English bone china cup, and an Irish Belleek Porcelain Tridacna textured shell cup in cream, yellow, and pale green. They were proudly displayed on her recently installed shelf—a beautiful relic made from an old train sleeper and exposed metal. She'd discovered it in a junkyard during one of her and Gina's stock trips to Spitalfields Market in London.

Just then, there was a knock at the back door. Since the only person who had access to that part of Lacey's property was Gina—her neighbor, employee, stand-in-mother, and best friend in Wilfordshire—that could only mean it was her.

Chester started barking with excited anticipation as Lacey went over to the barn-style back door and unlatched the top hatch. She swung it inward, revealing the beaming face of Gina.

Gina's cheeks were ruddy, her gray hair piled on top of her head in a messy bun. Beside her, her English shepherd, Boudica, sat obediently, panting in the summer heat.

"Just back from your walkies?" Lacey asked.

Chester immediately started yapping in response to the W-word.

"Oops, sorry, boy, I didn't mean you," Lacey told him, patting his head. Then to Boudica, she said, "I suppose you'll be wanting some water?"

She unlatched the bottom part of the door, and Boudica came bounding into the kitchen like she owned the place. She promptly began slurping water from Chester's bowl like she owned that, too. Chester paced over to her, his tail a-wagging, his nose a-sniffing, excited that his best friend had popped over, even if she was completely ignoring him and hogging the water bowl.

Lacey was excited to see her best friend, too. It hadn't even crossed her mind yet to ask why Gina had dropped around unannounced. She was so used to spending most of her waking hours with the older woman it seemed completely natural for her to just suddenly be in her kitchen. Which was why she was surprised when Gina said, "Don't you want to know why we're here?"

"For coffee?" Lacey guessed.

Gina shook her head.

"Tea?"

Gina scrunched her face as if to express that Lacey was getting closer.

"Long Island Iced Teas?" Lacey said, suggesting the boozy cocktail the two friends had recently acquired a taste for.

"No! To give you this!" Gina grinned widely and removed her satchel from her back, placing it on the kitchen counter. Then she opened it up and pulled out a china teacup.

"A Le Creuset!" Lacey exclaimed, immediately recognizing the iconic design.

"Now, I know it's not an antique," Gina began, "but ... "

"It's in the discontinued Elysees Yellow color!" Lacey exclaimed.

Gina nodded. "Exactly."

"Oh, Gina! I love it," Lacey cooed, as she took the cup and held it up to the light, turning it around in her hands like a precious diamond. "Did you know Marilyn Monroe had a set of Elysees Yellow that Sotheby's sold at auction for over twenty-five thousand dollars?"

Gina nodded. "Of course I do, darling. I work with you."

Lacey blushed. Of all the things to be a geek about! This must be how her Scotland-obsessed nephew, Frankie, felt every time he saw a person with ginger hair.

"It will look gorgeous on my shelf," Lacey told Gina, as she hurried over to add it to her collection. She was proud to now have four! "There. Doesn't that look wonderful?"

"Beautiful," Gina said. Then she removed a bottle of rum from her bag, followed by gin, tequila, and orange juice. "Now, did someone say Long Island Iced Teas?"

Lacey laughed. "Cocktails? I wish. But Tom is coming over today. I don't think it would be polite to be sozzled before he gets here. Take a rain check?"

"Rain," Gina replied, as she began reloading the liquors back into her bag of magic tricks. "I don't see much sign of that these days."

She was right. The late summer had been even more glorious than Lacey had expected for England. That old stereotype of it being a gray and rainy country had been well and truly dispelled.

Just then, Lacey heard her cell phone ping. Chester barked, as he always did, just in case she hadn't heard it. She picked up her phone from the counter and saw a message had come in from Tom. Her heart did its usual dum-durum-dum at the sight of her beau's name.

She opened the message and read.

*Lacey, I'm not going to be able to make it tonight. Something's come up at work. I'm so sorry! I'll make it up to you, I promise. Love you. Tom.*

"What?!" Lacey cried, her heart plummeting. "Tom's cancelling on me!"

She looked over at Gina, aghast. Her friend simply removed the array of liquors from her satchel one by one, lining them up on the kitchen counter.

"Make mine a double," Lacey muttered.

Gina topped up Lacey's Yellow Elysees Le Creuset cup with more Long Island Iced Tea from the pitcher, then lifted her Wedgwood Renaissance cream and gold cup from its saucer to her lips. They were sitting at the kitchen table by the large bay windows, watching the sun setting over the cliffs.

"You never told me what happened about your Canterbury lead," Gina said, looking solemnly over to Lacey. "Did you follow it up?"

At the mention of Canterbury, Lacey's stomach dropped. She'd recently made some inroads tracing her long-lost father, Francis, or Frank to his friends. She'd been following clues ever since moving to Wilfordshire, the place she last remembered her father being happy on a vacation many moons ago. Following leads from a variety of contacts in the antiques world, she'd learned that her father had, at some point in his two-decade absence from her life, put down roots in the English city of Canterbury. When he'd done so, Lacey couldn't be certain, though the clues seemed to suggest he'd been there recently, possibly still working in the world of antiquing, possibly even having opened a new store.

Of course, the logical thing for her to have done was travel to Canterbury, go to the first antiques store she found, and start asking around. But instead, she'd dragged her heels. There were other things she needed to do—sell the coin, run her business, decorate her home—but in her heart Lacey knew she was just making excuses. What if she went to Canterbury only to discover her father was no longer there? Or worse, what if she went and discovered he'd put down roots and had constructed a whole new comfortable life for himself without her in it?

"It was a dead end," Lacey fibbed. The last thing she needed was cajoling from Gina. As much as she loved the woman, she wasn't always the most patient person in the world, and Lacey needed more time to process it all.

Gina patted her hand. "I'm sorry, dear. Hopefully you'll find a new lead soon."

Lacey felt guilty for lying, but she forced a smile onto her lips. "Maybe it's for the best. I have a lot of things on my mind at the moment."

"Do you mean Tom?" Gina prompted.

Lacey let out a wistful sigh. "I just feel like ever since that first month, I've moved down his list of priorities," she lamented woefully. She was a little tipsy, splashing some cocktail from her cup onto the kitchen tiles as she gesticulated. Chester and Boudica immediately got into a nudging match to be the one who got to lick it up.

"What about the vacation?" Gina asked. "I'm sure he wouldn't have booked that if you weren't his priority?"

"Don't get me started on the vacation!" Lacey exclaimed. "You know our first romantic getaway was a complete disaster."

"I know it turned out to be a disaster, but that obviously wasn't Tom's intention. All those clues he sent you, and the lighthouse inn he booked. Those aren't the actions of someone who doesn't think of you as a priority."

Lacey slurped her drink. Gina was probably right, but she wanted to stew in her irritation for a little longer.

"And anyway," Gina continued, "it's not like he's always your priority either."

"Oh?" Lacey challenged. "What do you mean by that?"

"The Lodge," Gina said, eyebrows raised. "The whole time you were working on its interior design you didn't have time for anyone. Me included."

"Please," Lacey huffed. "Let's not drag up that old argument again. I need your unflagging support right now, Gina, not a lecture."

"I'm your friend," Gina said, patting her hand with equal parts affection and insistence. "That means I tell you hard truths about yourself and keep you in check. And in this situation, I think you and Tom both have a lot going on, and prioritizing your businesses over one another is sensible. Your business is forever, after all."

Lacey paused as Gina's words sunk in. Then she folded her arms. "Are you implying that our relationship is temporary?"

"I'm just saying it's still young and...." Gina stopped her sentence early.

"Go on," Lacey said. "It's young and ... "

Gina hesitated. Then she blurted, " ... .and weren't you one another's rebound relationship? I mean he was a couple years ahead of you in divorce terms, but you'd only just signed on the dotted line of your divorce papers if I recall correctly."

Lacey pursed her lips. "David and I separated months before the divorce was finalized. And I'm not a rebound for Tom, either. Taryn came between his ex-wife and me." She huffed. "We're very much in love."

"You are?" Gina said, sounding surprised.

"Yes!" Lacey exclaimed. "We told each other after Dover."

The switch in Gina was instant. "In that case, that changes everything! What's the point of being in a relationship if you're not one another's priority?"

Her complete about-face made Lacey dizzy. Or maybe that was the Long Island Iced Tea.

"The point," Lacey said, "is that this is hopefully a temporary blip. In a couple of weeks the tourist season ends and we should have more time to see one another."

Gina sat back and sipped her cocktail, a smirk on her lips. "And that, my dear," she said, "is called reverse psychology."

Lacey, realizing what Gina had done, rolled her eyes. "Very good," she said, dryly.

But she did appreciate it. Gina had managed to flip the conversation on its head, putting her in the position of defending her relationship.

Gina looked thoroughly proud of herself as she topped up their drinks. "So you just have one more week of summer to get through. And since it's the busiest, it'll be over in the blink of an eye and everything will go back to the way it was."

"Why will it be the busiest?" Lacey asked.

"Because of the festival."

"What festival?"

"The Summer Equestrian Festival!" Gina exclaimed. "Don't tell me no one's told you about it? It's the highlight of Wilfordshire's calendar."

Lacey shrugged. She was completely at a loss.

FIONA GRACE

Gina launched into an explanation. "It's when a bunch of rich horsey people descend on Wilfordshire for a week. A lot of businesses around here can double their takings just in that week alone!"

"And by rich horsey people you mean....?"

"Breeders, traders, racers, the whole shebang. The type of people who wear fascinators. Who drive Rolls Royces. Who buy their kids ponies, but get some other, poorer person's kids to muck them out!"

Lacey sat back in her seat and contemplated. Rich horsey people. Maybe this could be an opportunity to cash in big. Perhaps with another auction? Her nautical-themed one had been a hit. Would an equestrian-themed one be popular as well?

"When did you say the festival starts?" she asked Gina.

"It starts next week," the woman confirmed.

A smile inched across Lacey's lips. "In that case, I'd better get planning."

# Chapter Two

"**I**s that it?" Gina asked, peering over Lacey's shoulder at the writing pad scrawled with notes lying on the desk in front of her. "Your grand plan?"

It was the morning after the boozy night before, and the two women were in the antiques store, doing their best to tend to the steady stream of customers despite nursing pounding hangovers.

"My grand plan," Lacey confirmed, tapping the page with her pen. "I put aside a chunk of money from the sale of the gold coin which I can use to buy stock for an equestrian-themed auction. Tomorrow I'll go on a whistle-stop tour of Dorset to pick up some bits, bridles, stirrups, and spurs from a store in Bournemouth, then to a specialist leather store in Poole for some sandwich cases, canteens, and hip flasks, then finally to this cute little place in Weymouth where they sell prints and artworks."

"Mooth."

"What?"

"It's pronounced mooth, not mouth. Way-mooth. Born-mooth. The double O is the same as in book or nook or crook or hook or—"

"—I get it, I get it!" Lacey interjected, even though she was well aware she'd soon forget Gina's correction and absentmindedly revert back to a phonetic pronunciation. Pronouncing English place names was not one of her fortes. But to be fair to her, they had some really wacky spelling! Leicester? Try Lester! Worcestershire? Wooster-shear! Apparently, once you knew the rules it was pretty easy, but that all fell apart when Lacey confidently pronounced Cirencester "Sernster," only to discover she'd found the one exception to the rule, and it was pronounced how you'd guess: Siren-sester.

"Well, it sounds like you've got it all mapped out," Gina said with a sigh. "And Bournemouth is wonderful in the summer. There's a lovely sandy beach. A pier. Long cliff walks. Chester will love it."

The mournful edge to her tone was not lost on Lacey. Gina hated being left behind to man (or *wo*man) the store by herself when Lacey went off on adventures with Chester. It always made Lacey feel guilty. Then she'd have to remind herself she was the *boss* of the store, and that Gina was her *employee*, and that it was perfectly reasonable for her to do other things beyond standing behind a till and stacking shelves.

"I'll barely be gone a day," Lacey told her. "Then it will be all hands on deck to get the auction room ready. But while I'm gone, I have a very special project for you." Lacey had learned this technique after spending a day with her eight-year-old nephew, Frankie, in Dover—if he needed distracting, she'd just give him a "very important" job to do.

"Oh?" Gina asked, curiously, immediately falling for the bait.

Lacey smiled to herself. "I need you to call up the *Wilfordshire Weekly* and place the advertisement."

Gina grimaced. "Is that it?"

"AND," Lacey added, quickly thinking on her feet, "I need you to .... design a poster! Yes. That's it. I need you to design a poster for the community notice board and get it printed."

She hadn't originally been planning on printing posters for the auction at all, instead hoping an ad in the *Wilfordshire Weekly* would do most of the legwork, followed by passing foot traffic and word of mouth, but now she'd plucked the idea from her mind it seemed like a pretty good one. Her friend Suzy, who owned the Lodge B&B, always managed to get full bookings with some carefully targeted poster campaigns.

"Design the poster, eh?" Gina said, looking interested. "What do we think about that, Boo?" She looked down at her pup. Boudica whinnied her agreement. Gina turned back to Lacey. "It's a deal."

"Great!" Lacey said. "I'll be leaving tomorrow morning, so we can use the whole of Sunday to sort out the auction room. Do you think you'll be able to get the posters done by then?"

"Oh, easy-peasy," Gina said, already taking ownership of the task.

"And you know it's horse themed. So make sure there's a horse on it somewhere. No need to reinvent the wheel."

"Sure, sure, I've got it," Gina said, waving Lacey away.

Lacey wasn't entirely sure leaving the somewhat ditzy Gina in charge of the poster was a good idea but at least it would keep her busy. And now she was off the hook to spend a whole day in Dorset treasure hunting. How exciting!

"Do you think Tom would want to come with me?" Lacey said. "Since Dover was such a horrible disaster, maybe Dorset could be the do-over we need."

"You can ask him yourself," Gina said.

Lacey looked up at the same time as the bell over the door tinkled and Tom came rushing toward her. Lacey was surprised to see him so close to lunch time, his busiest hour. Maybe he'd come to apologize for bailing on her last night.

"What are you doing here?" Lacey asked, anticipation swirling inside of her.

"I need some change," Tom said, wafting a handful of twenty-pound notes at her as he went straight past her without stopping and promptly set about counting out coins from her till. "Tourists always pay with notes. Have you noticed that?"

She had, but that was beside the point. "I thought you were here to apologize," she said, deflating.

Tom was only half listening as he counted out change. "Apologize? What are you apologizing for?"

"Not me. You! You cancelled on me last night."

Tom's head darted up. He immediately stopped what he was doing. "Oh! Oh, Lacey, of course. I'm so sorry!" He abandoned his pile of coins and finally focused on her. He rubbed her arm tenderly. "I really am sorry for canceling on you."

"What happened?" Lacey asked. It wasn't like Tom to be so unreliable.

"Just boring work stuff," he said. "I had a bride call up in floods of tears canceling her wedding cake because her father was being taken to hospital with a suspected heart attack. I'd almost finished frosting the whole thing, so to cut my losses, I sliced the cake up and sold the pieces.

Only the bride called back a few hours later to tell me the wedding was back on because her dad was fine; it was just indigestion! So then I had to make a whole other cake."

"Well, as happy as I am for the bride and her digestively challenged father," Lacey said, "it was a total bummer for me."

"I know," Tom said, caressing her cheek tenderly. "I get it. I'll make it up to you, I promise. Just one more crazy week to get through, then things can go back to normal."

Lacey couldn't stay mad at him. He was clearly stressed. Tom usually enjoyed the buzz of his work at the patisserie, but right now it seemed to be frazzling him.

"The horse festival keeping you busy, huh?" Lacey asked.

Tom nodded. "This morning a kid climbed on the window display and knocked over the macaron racing horse I'd made for the festival. I've been trying to rebuild it all morning but the place has been so rammed, I've not gotten the chance yet."

Lacey peeped through the window and across the street to Tom's famous macaron display. Right now, it was a headless horse. She couldn't help but laugh. "Oh dear."

Gina guffawed. "Looks like the mafia got to it."

"Yes, I've heard that one," Tom said wearily. "At least five times. Because every other customer makes some joke about it." He put on a silly voice, and said, "'Someone should report you to the RSPCA.' 'Patisserie? I thought this was the butcher's.' Et cetera."

He went back to counting out his change.

Lacey leaned her backside against the counter, watching him. "I guess now's not a good time to invite you along on a day trip tomorrow."

Tom looked up, his expression anguished. "Tomorrow?"

"I'm going to hold another themed auction for the festival," she explained. "I'm planning on a stock run in Dorset."

"Another auction?" Tom said, smiling. "That's great. And I wish I could, but my gingerbread horses won't bake themselves."

"That's okay," Lacey said, failing to hide her disappointment. "Chester can be my companion."

Chester's ears twitched at the sound of his name.

"I'm sorry, Lacey," Tom said earnestly. "Once the festival is over we can take as many day trips to Dorset as your heart desires."

Lacey felt dubious about that. Until Tom hired some decent staff, there'd always be something that took up all his attention.

"Hey, I have an idea," Tom said suddenly, clicking his fingers. "Why don't you take my van? It'll give you more space for all your purchases."

He flashed her a hopeful smile. He was obviously trying to help but his van wasn't much of a substitute for spending time with him, in Lacey's opinion.

"Don't you need it?" she asked.

Tom shook his head and rummaged in his pocket for his keys. "It's all yours," he said. "Just bring it back in one piece. I'd better get back to the patisserie and deal with that headless horse."

He gave Lacey a quick peck, then hurried off, clinking from all the change in his pockets.

Lacey stood holding the van keys, feeling a bit like a child who'd been fobbed off with her parents' car. The whole interaction had felt extremely disappointing but Lacey decided not to dwell on it. Tomorrow she'd be setting off on a brand new adventure and who knew what exciting treasures she would find?

# CHAPTER THREE

Saturday morning arrived in a blaze of late summer sunshine. Lacey set off early to make sure she got ahead of the traffic. Tom's van was stuffy, so she cracked the windows and enjoyed the breeze as she drove.

She'd chosen to take the long route to Bournemouth, avoiding the A-roads and motorways in favor of the countryside roads. There was nothing quite like a drive in the English countryside, on winding single-lane roads slicing through fields and hillsides, especially on a bright summer's day. Lacey would never tire of it, and was delighted as she drove past sheep-dotted grassland and fields of rippling wheat, as excited for the countryside as she was for the upcoming treasure hunt.

She reached Bournemouth, and the quiet country roads became a thing of the past as she was suddenly thrust into the busy seaside town, and all the tarmac and traffic that came with it. A lot of people had obviously decided to visit Bournemouth beach this weekend, and it took Lacey a long time to find somewhere to park the bulky van. She ended up quite far along the cliffs, by a dated cafe and playground filled with wooden equipment and an abundance of children.

Lacey killed the engine and took a moment. At thirty-nine, she knew her window for making a decision about having a family was quickly closing. She'd been steadfast against it, back when she lived in New York City with her now ex-husband, David. But since moving to England, where the pace of life was slower and things in her life had begun to align, there had been a shift in her attitude. Spending time with Frankie and discovering she was actually pretty good at it had also prompted her to rethink her position. That, and her impending fortieth birthday, which she was trying to forget about, though it was fast approaching.

Chester broke Lacey from her reverie by pawing at the door and whining loudly. He'd enjoyed the drive here, sticking his head out the window, but was obviously eager to get out and explore the gorgeous sandy beach below.

"You know, who needs kids when they've got a dog?"

Chester barked his agreement.

They hopped down from the vehicle and headed toward the path that sloped all the way down from the cliffs to the seafront. A whole cluster of paragliders were taking it in turns to launch into the air, float over the sea in a queue of bright fabric wings toward the pier, then loop back around again and land on the cliff. Chester barked excitedly as a man with a rainbow sail took to the sky.

"I wonder if they make tandem gliders for dogs," Lacey mused aloud to Chester as they passed.

They headed down the slope and reached the beach, which was bustling with families, groups of teenagers, old folks picnicking, dog walkers, volleyball players, hula-hoopers ... practically every type of person one could expect to see. The calm waters were full of canoeists, kayakers, paddle boarders, and sunbathers on inflatable rafts, while yachts and speedboats crisscrossed the deeper waters beyond the jetties. Gina was right; Bournemouth beach was far busier than Wilfordshire beach, but Lacey loved the buzz of it all. Not to mention the golden sand, which was much vaster than the beach at Wilfordshire.

Lacey couldn't resist; she slipped off her shoes and sank her feet into it. Meanwhile, Chester ran up to the sea and started snapping at the waves as if trying to catch them.

"Ice cream!" a voice called. "Ice cream!"

Lacey turned to see a man pushing a refrigerated trolley along the beach. He gestured to her. "You look like a lady who needs an ice cream."

"I couldn't possibly," Lacey told him. "Every time I eat ice cream my dog gets jealous."

"Perhaps he'd like to sample one of my frozen dog treats?"

"Frozen dog treats?!" Lacey exclaimed. "That sounds very niche."

"Are you kidding me? Ninety percent of people in this town own a dog or two. My frozen pupsicles sell like hotcakes. Or cold cakes." He grinned.

"What are they made of?" Lacey asked skeptically. Dairy was an absolute no-no for Chester, as was anything containing chocolate or sugar substitutes, which were toxic and potentially fatal for dogs.

"There are two flavors to choose from," the man said, producing bone-shaped frozen treats from his cooler. In his left hand was a watery-looking orange one. In his right, a watery green one. "We have pureed carrot on the left, and pureed honeydew melon on the right," he said. "Both vet-approved recipes."

Chester barked.

"Well, in that case, I'll take one of each," Lacey said.

"And a tropical fruit popsicle for the human?" He waved a very juicy-looking popsicle at her. "So you don't get jealous?"

Lacey chuckled. "A tropsicle? Fine, I'll take it."

She exchanged money for the frozen treats, then she and Chester slowly meandered along the beach devouring them. Mango, pineapple, and watermelon flavors flooded Lacey's taste buds. The blend wasn't overly sweet, and the iciness was refreshingly welcome.

"How were yours?" Lacey asked Chester, noting the sticky residue on his muzzle. "Tasty, I presume," she chuckled.

Just then, Lacey spotted an old Art Deco–style building in the near distance. It was the shopping emporium where the horse supplies store was located, standing on the top of the hill with views over the sea and the rest of Bournemouth town.

Excited, Lacey licked the sugary goo from her fingers, slipped her shoes back on, and hastened her pace off the beach and onto the sidewalk. Chester followed, his coat covered in sand and his face wet from sea water.

They reached the building, which had been a cinema back in its heyday and was now filled with small pop-up shops. Inside, it reminded Lacey of the London markets she visited with Gina, from the kooky Greenwich market, to the bustling food market of Brixton, the historic Covent Garden market, to the Borough food market under the eaves of the train station. Lacey loved the quirks of English architecture, where new builds seemed in short supply, grand old buildings were repurposed for other uses such as undercover markets or shopping centers, and no space was too small for a pop-up craft store.

The market here was like its own town within the town. Myriad food stalls offered street food from every corner of the globe. Lacey's mouth watered as the scents of Ethiopian injera flatbread and South Korean soybean stew with kimchi cabbage wafted into her nostrils, before they were overpowered by the pungent floral smells of a packaging-free organic soap stall, where huge bricks of brightly colored soaps were arranged into a pyramid. She carried on, passing the distinct mothball smell of a stall selling vintage thrift clothing, on past a surfboard shop, before finally losing her willpower when she reached a vegan cupcake stall. A dark chocolate, peanut butter, and oatmeal breakfast muffin gave her a small taste of heaven.

She weaved through the busy stalls, realizing she could have easily lost the entire day just here, before finding the equestrian supply store she was looking for.

It was clean inside. The carpet was an appropriate racehorse green. The display cabinets were made from wood and brass. There was a calming uniformity to the place.

Lacey approached the counter and introduced herself to the woman behind it, whose curly brown hair was pulled back into a bushy ponytail.

"Belinda?" Lacey said, offering her hand. "We spoke on the phone yesterday. I'm Lacey, the auctioneer from Devon."

"I remember," Belinda said with a grin, as she shook Lacey's extended hand. "You're from Wilfordshire where they host the Summer Equestrian Festival."

"That's right. Do you know it?"

"Of course! I've gone a few times in the past to set up a stall, but the cost of a hotel, petrol for the car, and the table fee for the market all adds up. I can turn a bigger profit keeping the store here open. It's a shame to miss it though. Always such a fun time."

It seemed to Lacey as if everyone in the country knew about Wilfordshire's famous horse festival, apart from her.

The woman looked at Chester. "And who is this gorgeous fellow?" she gushed, coming out from behind the counter to pet his head. She was, quite appropriately, wearing jodhpurs.

Chester barked hello.

"This is my trusty companion, Chester," Lacey said. "We just had some frozen dog treats on the beach."

"It's lovely down there, isn't it?"

"I'll say. As much as I adore Wilfordshire's wild, craggy beach, I am partial to the feel of warm sand between my toes."

Belinda smiled. "I suppose you'll be wanting to see my antique stock?"

She led Lacey to the items she'd set aside for her to peruse. There were bits, bridles, stirrups, and spurs galore. Lacey immediately began inspecting them for any hidden gems.

"I must say," Belinda said as Lacey worked, "I'm glad there's an antiques store in Wilfordshire again."

"Again?" Lacey asked, somewhat absentmindedly, since her attention was on the task at hand. She'd found some very interesting bridles and bits for infantry mounted officers and military cavalries.

"There was one years back," Belinda continued. "Must've been twenty or so now. It was run by this beautiful, glamorous woman. I think she was a countess, or baroness, or something similar. There was some blue blood in her, or at least that's what the rumors say."

"How interesting," Lacey murmured, putting down the pair of nineteenth-century Latin American spurs she'd been inspecting and moving on to some fifteenth-century Gothic ones.

Belinda continued her story. "She was disowned by her family for choosing to work and falling in love with an ordinary man." She sounded wistful at the romance of it all.

"She sounds like quite a character," Lacey said, discovering a rare pair of silver French spurs with a unique phoenix design. She looked up. "These are all fantastic. I'll take them all."

"Really?" Belinda asked, sounding surprised. "I've had some of these for years without even a hint of interest from customers!"

Lacey smiled. This was the game of antiques, the thrill of it. One trader may be holding on to goods for years without a market to sell them to, only for another seller confident in their customer pool to turn a profit for both parties. Most of Belinda's stock were low-ticket items, the type that could sit around for years gathering dust, only to sell in dribs and drabs for twenty to thirty pounds. But as companion pieces to a themed auction they could help push up the price of the higher-ticket items. The pair of unique silver French spurs could fetch hundreds of pounds if the right bidder was present on auction day. Lacey wouldn't usually take such a big risk, but she felt confident it would pay off—provided that Gina's claims that a whole bunch of rich horsey people were about to descend on Wilfordshire were accurate. And by offering to take the entire lot off Belinda's hands, she got a much better deal overall.

Lacey left the Bournemouth store with a big box in her arms and a big smile on her face, thrilled that her treasure hunt had gotten off to such a good start.

The next stop on the whistle-stop tour of Dorset was Poole, just a twenty-minute drive along the coast. Turned out the van had actually been a very good idea after all. It was already far more full of stock than Lacey had anticipated, and she'd only been to one store so far! There was still the specialist leather store and the art store to visit.

In the rearview mirror, Lacey assessed the amount of bits, bridles, stirrups, and spurs she'd just bought, excited by her haul, before her gaze flicked to Chester. He was sitting straight backed and self-important in the back seat, the wind ruffling through his ears.

"Have I gone a little over the top?" she asked him.

He tipped his head to the side, as if she was talking nonsense.

"Are you sure?"

He barked.

"You're right," she said, reassured. "This is way lower risk than if I was just buying up a bunch of themed stuff without the customer base. In fact, it's hardly a risk at all if Gina and Tom are to be believed."

She paused at the mention of Tom. *He* should be the one on this trip with her, really, reassuring her over her purchases rather than a dog, as wonderful as Chester was at it. But instead he was completely consumed by work. He had Paul, the hapless intern, to help lighten the load somewhat, but after Lucia left for a new job at Suzy's guest house, he hadn't hired anyone new. Why he hadn't hired another staff member to help out for the rest of the busy tourist season, Lacey just couldn't comprehend. Especially considering he was well aware of the upcoming Summer Equestrian Festival. It was almost as if he was sabotaging their relationship.

"Did I tell him I loved him too soon, Chester?" she asked her confidant. "Does he think he can rest on his laurels now because he's got me?" She started to grow more and more anxious. "Are we already in a rut? It's only been a few months. This is supposed to be our honeymoon period, where we're giddy and everything feels perfect! But here I am playing second fiddle to a patisserie!"

Chester whined.

Lacey pursed her lips. "Okay. Maybe I'm projecting a bit."

He whined again.

"All right, okay, I get it. I'm expecting Tom to be like David, even though they're nothing alike. That's why I fell for him, because of how different he is from David. I'm just dissatisfied because I want to spend more time with him and I can't." She reached over and petted Chester's velvety ears. "Thanks for being such a good listener, boy."

Half an hour later, Lacey coasted the van over the crest of a hill, and the sea opened up before her. Down below she saw Poole Harbour, which was nothing like what she'd been expecting. To her, a harbor was a man-made construction. Poole Harbour, on the other hand, appeared to be naturally occurring; the estuary for several large rivers. The water was extremely shallow, and there were land masses dotted around within it. Yachts, cruise boats, and large passenger ferries trawled through the waters.

"Keep your eyes peeled for the leather shop," Lacey told Chester.

She followed the road that ran parallel to the harbor. It was lined with cool seafront eateries and restaurants, their outside seating areas completely full of weekend revelers soaking up the last few weeks of the summer sun in anticipation of it giving way to fall.

Fall. Lacey's favorite season. She was excited to see what England looked like once the leaves turned orange, red, and brown. Wilfordshire would most certainly look stunning, and if the High Street marked the change in season with bunting (as it had with both spring and summer), it would be even prettier. Lacey's mind went into a romantic flight of fantasy as she pictured enjoying bonfires and toasted marshmallows with Tom, sipping on warm spiced cider and munching on roasted chestnuts.

*If he can spare a moment for me, that is,* Lacey thought glumly, her romantic picture shattering in her mind like a cracked mirror.

She couldn't help but feel dubious about Tom's claims he'd be more available once the busy summer tourist season was over. After all, there were three holidays to get through—Harvest Festival, Halloween, and Guy Fawkes' Night—before they headed into the busy Christmas season preparations. People would want cakes and cookies for every one of them, not to mention some elaborate macaron window display. If there was one thing Lacey had learned about celebrations in the UK, it was that there was always an associated dish, and Tom would feel compelled to create a unique version of it to put on sale. She could already imagine the amount of work he'd put into his Halloween-themed gingerbread men after having witnessed his Easter gingerbread bunnies and the Equestrian Festival's gingerbread horses. Knowing Tom, he'd probably construct an entire gingerbread haunted house! And he wouldn't settle for selling his usual croissants and cakes, either. Tom was too dedicated to his craft for that. He'd toil away for hours creating new recipes for cinnamon spiced apple Danishes and pumpkin muffins. It was highly unlikely he'd find any time for her at all.

Suddenly, Chester started barking, and Lacey snapped out of her anxious ruminations to see the leather store was upon them. She'd almost driven right past it, she'd been so lost in her thoughts.

"Thanks, Chester," she said to her pup.

He barked proudly.

She pulled the van to the curb and cut the engine. Then she and Chester hopped out into the glorious sunshine and headed inside the leather store.

It was much larger inside than Lacey had been expecting. A set of steep wooden stairs to her left indicated there was a whole other floor of goods in addition to the floor she'd entered into, which seemed to stretch back forever. A quick glance around showed Lacey that the store stocked both new and vintage leather, everything from cowboy boots to Moroccan sandals imported straight from Marrakech. The smell was a little over-powering—Lacey preferred the dusty, metallic smell of antiques—and it was very dark. The narrow aisles were absolutely crammed with leather goods. Purses hung from the ceilings, and there were numerous racks stuffed with jackets and the sort of skin-tight pants Lacey was certain had gone out of fashion in the '80s. It was so crammed in the store, Lacey didn't even know where to begin looking for the antique items she'd come for.

She squeezed her way through the aisles, negotiating her way past a mannequin display of a man in a suede suit and a woman in a dominatrix outfit (complete with whip), before finding herself at the raised counter behind which stood the clerk. He was an older guy with a long gray beard and black, tassled leather waistcoat over a white T tucked into pale blue jeans. Lacey imagined him as a motorbike-riding, guitar-wielding rock star. Or a retired one, at the very least.

She looked up at him. "Could you show me where to find your horse riding equipment? It said on your website you also sell vintage sandwich cases, canteens, and hip flasks."

"If it's made of leather, we'll have at least one somewhere," he said in a voice that was far more gentle than his appearance would suggest. "Come with me."

Lacey followed the man, who was shorter than her once he'd stepped down from the counter. He moved his skinny frame deftly through the aisles. Lacey had to hurry to keep up. He obviously knew the store very well, and Lacey guessed that he was the owner.

They reached the steep wooden staircase and ascended. It creaked under them. Lacey discovered the next floor was just as full of stock as the ground floor.

"You have an impressive range of stock," she said as she surveyed the room in front of her.

"I've been here for thirty years now," he replied. "I've accumulated a lot in that time."

"I can tell."

He led her toward the back of the store.

"So are you a rider?" the man asked as they went.

"Motorcycles?" Lacey asked, assuming he was referring to his garb.

He laughed. "No. Horses."

"Oh!" Lacey laughed too. "No, I'm an antiquer and auctioneer. I'm holding an equestrian-themed auction, hence the interest."

"Cool," the man said. "I'm into vintage, as you can probably tell, but I'm kind of clueless when it comes to antiques."

They reached the section of the store devoted to horse-riding and Lacey saw that all the new and vintage pieces were mixed up together. He was right when he'd said he was clueless; most of the handwritten labels said such undescriptive things as *old bag*. It was going to take a very long time to work her way through it all.

"Is this the sort of stuff you were looking for?" he asked.

"Uh-huh."

"Are you sure? Because you look really disappointed."

"I'm sorry," Lacey said. She softened her features, realizing as she did just how hard she'd been frowning. "I'm just thinking that it will take me a long time to find everything I'm looking for."

"I can help," the man said. "You can teach me a thing or two about antiques as we go."

"Okay," Lacey said, taking him up on his offer. "Thanks." She got out her cell and showed him the photographs of the types of items she wanted. "These are sandwich cases, or saddle canteens. They clip onto the saddle, so the rider can bring lunch with them."

"I've got about a million of those," he said, before disappearing down another aisle.

Lacey looked at Chester and shrugged. Maybe this wasn't going to take that long after all, with a helper.

The man returned a few moments later pushing a large trolley labeled *various satchels,* then tipped it up and dumped the entire contents on the floor, in a mound of leather.

"You weren't kidding," Lacey said, feeling giddy, like a child who'd just been surrounded by toys. She sat down on the floor next to the pile ready to begin hunting for treasure. "The next thing I'm looking for are saddle flasks, like these." She handed him her cell phone for the reference picture and off he went.

Lacey started rifling through the mountain of bags, setting aside the ones that were in poor condition and the ones that were knock-off remakes, in the hopes of finding a few that would be suitable for her auction. Then she found just the thing: a dark tan, Swaine-Brigg sandwich case with the original silver tin inside. Both bag and tin were in perfect condition, and Lacey was confident she'd fetch a few hundred pounds for them at auction. She placed the bag in her keep pile and continued sifting. Next, she found a curved sandwich case. Inside, stamped on the doeskin lining in black ink, it read, "James Dixon & Sons, Sheffield," with a date: 1879. And, once again, this one had its original silver sandwich tin in pristine condition. She added it to her keep pile.

Next she found a Champion & Wilton sidesaddle case in tan leather, complete with flask and sandwich tin, swiftly followed by a horse rider's shoulder bag, curved to fit comfortably against the body with matching curved sandwich tin and hip flask.

"Chester, this is like Christmas," Lacey gushed as she added it to her pile.

Chester lifted his head sleepily from his paws and yawned.

"I'm glad you're having fun," the store clerk said, returning with a large box.

"Are those all flasks?" Lacey asked, surprised.

"I could only find a couple of flasks," he said. "But I thought you might want to see these." He pulled a boot from the box.

Lacey leapt up. It was very distinctly a WWI-era cavalry riding boot. "Please tell me you have the matching boot in there?" she said, her excitement increasing.

He grinned. "There are about ten pairs in here."

He lowered the box so Lacey could see inside. Ten pairs of riding boots, all in a saleable condition.

"You're right," she said, smiling. "I did want to see these!"

As Lacey inspected the boots for wear and tear, the clerk took a seat. "So what made you specialize in riding equipment?" he asked. "If you're not a horse rider."

"I'm holding an auction for the Summer Equestrian Festival," Lacey explained. "I'm from Wilfordshire."

"Wilfordshire?" the man asked with an air of recognition. "I knew an antiquer from Wilfordshire."

"Was it the countess?" Lacey said with a chuckle as she recalled Belinda's story. "I've heard some interesting tales about her."

"No, it was a man," he replied. "An American, actually like you. Come to think of it, he looked a bit like you, too."

Lacey felt the blood drain from her face instantly. "Was his name Frank?"

"That's it! Frank the Yank!" He clicked his fingers and grinned. "Do you know him?"

# CHAPTER FOUR

L acey tried to compose herself. She was overwhelmed by the urge to
fire a million questions at the leather store clerk, but didn't want to
stress the man out by revealing that he may be talking about her long-
lost father. She tried to play it casual, as if Frank was just a contact they
shared.

"I know Frank through work," she said. "You?"

"Same," the leather store man said. "Frank toured around the country
for his stock. London. Poole. Wilfordshire. But am I right in thinking his
store was located in Canterbury?"

"Yes, I believe so," Lacey said, breathlessly.

Canterbury. There it was again, the lead Xavier had discovered. The
lead that had been tangentially confirmed by the message written in the
front pages of *The Canterbury Tales* from a man named Frank to his
lover. Add to that Lacey's own memories from her childhood summer
vacation in Wilfordshire, where her mother refused to come and Naomi
broke a statue in an antiques store run by a beautiful woman, and it was
all starting to build a coherent picture.

Her heart started pounding. "I don't suppose you're still in touch with
Frank, are you?" she asked.

The man shook his head. "I think he moved away quite recently. Last
I heard, his store had closed down."

Lacey felt a sudden, sharp pain in her chest, like she'd just jumped
into the icy ocean. "He's not there anymore? Are you sure? I know his
New York City store shut down, but I didn't realize his one in Canterbury
had as well." She swallowed the hard, panicked lump that was forming
in her throat.

"Yeah. Real shame. He was a lovely bloke. I wonder where he is now."

He paused, leaving the question Lacey had spent many years agonizing over lingering between them.

Then, "I'm surprised you know Frank from work," he said. "You look far too young to be a work acquaintance! I wouldn't have put you a day over forty."

Lacey forced a smile. What good would come of her telling this man that he was right, that she was too young to have known Frank in a work capacity because she was his daughter, not a business associate, and that he'd abandoned her as a child?

"I don't suppose you know where he went?" Lacey asked. She was doing her absolute best to remain calm, but she could hear that her voice was trembling.

"Beats me," the man said, shrugging. "Someone at Sawyer's might know."

"Sawyer's?" Lacey asked.

"Sawyer & Sons. The big auction house in Dorchester. You can't be a contact of Frank's and not know Sawyer's! He was in there every weekend for a time."

"It must've slipped my mind."

Lacey could hardly assimilate all this new information. To learn her father had opened a store in Canterbury only to have recently moved on felt bitterly cruel, almost worse than never knowing he'd had a store there in the first place. And now to have a glimpse into the life he'd lived in England—visiting Sawyer & Sons auction house every weekend—felt strangely intrusive. It sounded as if he'd just fallen back into the same routine and lifestyle he'd left behind in New York City, only this one hadn't involved a wife or children. Was that the only thing he'd needed to change about his life? Were they the only reason he'd left?

"I have a flyer," the man added, taking a glossy pamphlet down from a notice board display and handing it to Lacey. "It lists all of Sawyer & Sons' auctions this year."

Lacey scanned the pamphlet. The map on the back showed the auction house's Dorchester location was only a short detour from her next planned stop of Weymouth. It wouldn't add too much to her journey to swing by, although she may come away from it with an even bigger bruise on her heart.

She decided it was a risk she would have to take. She'd chosen not to detour to Canterbury while she'd been on vacation in Dover nearby, and that decision may very well have cost her the only real lead she had for her father.

She bought her wares and thanked the leather store owner for all his help, then headed to the van with Chester. Once she'd secured her stock in the van, she called her store to check up.

"How's it all going?" she said into her cell phone.

"Busy," came Gina's voice in her ear. "How's the treasure hunt?"

Lacey mulled over whether or not to tell Gina about what she'd learned about her father. She came down on the side of not. Speaking it out loud would make it feel more real, and she wasn't ready for that just yet.

"More fruitful than I anticipated," she said, evasively.

"Well, I just got off the blower with the printers," Gina said. "Turns out they're closed tomorrow so the only time they could print the posters was today, so I just went ahead and gave them the green light."

The last thing on Lacey's mind right now was a poster, what with everything she'd just learned about her father. "That's fine. I trust you. As long as there's a horse on the poster, I don't need to see it first."

"Yes, yes. There's a horse. Of sorts."

Lacey's eyelids closed in time to the sinking feeling in her chest. "Of sorts? What does that mean?"

"Well, I got the picture off the internet," Gina explained. "I searched for 'racing horse' and got the image off the tab. So I didn't go to the actual website."

Lacey didn't like where this was going. "Go on ... "

"It was only afterward that I realized the picture was from a rescue site, a charity for horses that have been retired. You know, put out to pasture. So it *is* a horse, just a very old, decrepit one."

Lacey sighed. Good thing the task was just a distraction. "Hopefully no one notices," she said. "Look, I have to go now. I'm taking a small detour. There's an auction house a few miles out of my way that I want to visit. See if I can make a new contact."

"Of course," Gina replied ruefully. Lacey could practically hear her roll her eyes. "So will I be balancing the till and closing up tonight?"

That familiar swirl of guilt rolled in Lacey's stomach. She had to remind herself that in this context, Gina was her employee. Asking her to perform routine tasks was well within her pay bracket. "If I'm not back to do it, then yes."

"Fine," Gina sighed.

Lacey ended the call and looked at Chester. "Honestly, sometimes the way she speaks to me you'd think I didn't even pay her! Or give her that big hydroponic system she'd been harping on about for months."

She rolled her eyes and turned the key in the ignition. The van sputtered to life. As she pulled back onto the harbor road, heading toward Dorchester, she looked at the leather store in her wing mirror. She'd never expected when she entered that she'd be leaving with something far more precious than antiques: a solid lead on her father.

# CHAPTER FIVE

The Sawyer & Sons auction house was located in the sort of English country manor Lacey's mom and sister would kill to live in. Ivy climbed its weathered red bricks, surrounding the white-framed windows on its second floor. Expensive SUVs filled the gravel lot out front. Lacey couldn't help but blush as Tom's ugly van noisily puttered into place beside them.

Lacey double-checked the pamphlet the leather store man had given her.

"There's an auction on today," she told Chester, glancing up at the van's digital clock. "It starts in fifteen minutes. We'll have to hurry if we want to catch one of the Sawyers."

She hopped out of the van. Chester jumped out after her. Together, they climbed the stone steps and entered in through the large doors of the manor house.

The foyer was so grand and so full of people, Lacey felt like she'd walked into a theater rather than an auction house. Sawyer's was clearly a super-classy establishment. She couldn't help but feel a little self-conscious in her casual clothes.

A sign above her head indicated that the office for payments and collections was straight ahead. *Please allow five minutes between purchase and collection*, it said. The auction room was through doors on the right, so Lacey headed left into the showroom where all the upcoming auction's lots were on display.

The showroom was as large as a ballroom and packed full of beautiful antiques. Two banquet-style tables ran through the center of the room, displaying ornaments, jewelry, porcelain, and art, while large pieces of furniture encircled the perimeter.

Lacey felt a hitch of delight in her chest. It was an antique dealer's dream come true. The sort of place she aspired to run one day. The sort of place her father would quickly lose himself in . . .

A heaviness settled on her shoulders as she remembered why she'd come here in the first place; not to hunt for antiques, but to hunt for clues as to her father's whereabouts.

She scanned the room. A smartly dressed man stood at the far end of the hall. His formal black suit immediately gave him away as a Sawyer & Sons auctioneer.

Lacey took several paces in the direction of the man, only for him to be approached by a customer. She halted her advance. Chester quirked his head at her quizzically.

"I don't want to interrupt him when he's dealing with a customer," she explained.

Chester huffed. It was as if he knew the real reason she'd stopped her approach was to buy more time, that she'd just jumped on the first excuse not to speak to the man. Because if he did indeed know the fate of her father, then what came next? The fear of knowing what had happened to her father seemed suddenly worse than the uncertainty she'd gotten used to all these years.

The suited man headed off with the customer to attend to their query.

"Let's look at the furniture until he's free," Lacey said hurriedly, pacing away in the opposite direction.

Chester gave her another huff and trotted after her.

Lacey was gazing absentmindedly at a writing bureau in walnut wood when a voice from beside her said, "What a gorgeous dog."

She looked over to see a man crouched down beside Chester, petting him. He was fairly smartly dressed in a sand-colored suit jacket, white shirt, and beige slacks. His hair was dark blond and curly.

"I'm a big fan of the Border collie," he added, looking up at Lacey with twinkling blue eyes. He smiled, and dimples appeared in his cheeks.

"He's an English shepherd," Lacey told him.

The man started to laugh, his pearly teeth on show. "Ah, you're American. Over here we call them Border collies."

"You do?" Lacey said, surprised. "I'll have to remember that." She could use it to impress Gina once she was back in Wilfordshire.

"They're a lovely breed, aren't they?" the man continued. "I got a collie when I was a kid just because my name is Colin." He chuckled. "But it ended up being a great decision! I've had a collie companion ever since."

As he ruffled Chester's fur, Lacey glanced back over her shoulder, searching for the Sawyer son. She found him, standing alone once again. Now was her chance to speak to him about her father. But Lacey felt too anxious to even move.

"I'm sorry," Colin said, suddenly. "I'm talking your ear off, aren't I?"

"Not at all," Lacey said, turning back, embarrassed for being rude and grateful for an excuse not to take action. "You were telling me about your collie companion."

Colin stopped petting Chester and stood. He was tall and slender. Lacey guessed he was in his mid – to late forties.

"Stella," he said. "She's at home. She's far too old for these long days out now unfortunately. But she used to love an auction in her youth." He smiled again. "What's your dog's name?"

"Chester," she said, watching as her pooch started pacing around the base of the walnut bureau, nose first, sniffing centuries' worth of interesting scents. "I adopted him when I moved to the UK. Actually, he adopted me."

"And is this his way of sniffing out a bargain?" Colin joked, as Chester began his second lap of the bureau.

Lacey chuckled. "He likes to think he's helping."

Just then, a voice sounded over the public address system. "Ladies and gentlemen, if you could please take your seats now, the auction will commence in five minutes."

Lacey looked over to the spot she'd last seen the Sawyer son. He'd gone. She'd missed her chance to talk to him. She'd been too distracted by her chat with Colin. Or, in honesty, she'd let herself be distracted by Colin because she was too nervous to follow the lead on her father.

"After you," Colin said, gesturing to the door that led out to the foyer.

She headed out, Chester trotting beside her, trying to work out what to do next. The auction was going to last for hours. She couldn't wait until the end to speak to the black-suited man. Then she remembered the sign in the foyer. She'd only have to wait five minutes after the sale of the first item before there was someone in the office she could speak to. So she headed into the auction room to kill the five minutes.

Colin gestured to a seat and Lacey took it. Chester nudged his way past her legs and lay at her feet with a large yawn.

"Someone's sleepy," Colin commented as he took the seat beside her.

"We set out early this morning," Lacey explained, before suddenly realizing she'd only had one coffee at breakfast and it was now almost lunch time! She yawned before she could stop herself.

"You must be sleepy too," Colin said. "Let me fetch you a coffee. They have refreshments at the side."

"You don't have to do that," Lacey tried to say, but her yawn had turned into a comically protracted one she wasn't able to speak through.

It was too late. Colin disappeared to fetch the coffee.

The seats started filling up quickly, and a group of elderly people started shuffling along the row toward her.

"This seat is taken," Lacey said to an old woman coming up on her left-hand side.

"What?" the woman said loudly.

"This seat is taken," Lacey tried again. She noticed the woman had a hearing aid in, so she patted the seat to emphasize her point.

"Thank you, dear!" the woman shouted, clearly having misunderstood and promptly sitting in Colin's seat.

Lacey turned to the right just as a man on crutches with a broken leg sat in the other spare space beside her.

She stood, looking around for another pair of seats, only to discover the auction room had almost completely filled up. At the same time, Colin returned with the coffees. He took one look either side of her at the old woman with the hearing aid and the injured man with crutches before laughing, giving her a playful shrug, and abandoning the coffee on the side table. He took a seat further up the hall.

Lacey sank back down, surprised by just how disappointed she felt to not be sitting next to Colin for the auction.

*Because it's nice to have company,* she told herself, sternly.

The black-suited man took to the stage, and his microphone squeaked as he spoke into it. "Good afternoon, ladies and gentleman. I'm Jonty Sawyer and I'd like to welcome you all to this weekend's auction. We're starting with two very striking artworks by the famous Mexican muralist, David Alfaro Siqueiros, both previously exhibited at the Memorial Art Gallery in New York."

The assistant carefully placed the first painting onto the display easel. It was a gorgeous interpretation of a horse, in black swirls.

"Here we have Horse & Rider, which was painted with shoe polish," Jonty Sawyer said. The assistant placed the second picture on the display easel. It was an oil painting of a man on a horse in bright reds and browns. "The second is this vibrant oil painting."

Lacey was stunned. They were both gorgeous pieces, and absolutely perfect for the clientele she was expecting to attend her own auction. She'd not expected to actually want anything at the auction, but suddenly found herself readying to bid on them, her heart pounding with excited anticipation.

"We'll start the bidding at five hundred pounds," Jonty Sawyer announced.

Lacey raised her hand immediately.

"Five hundred pounds," Jonty confirmed, pointing at her.

A hand further up the hall went up.

"Five fifty?" he asked, then with a nod, affirmed, "Five fifty."

He looked back at Lacey. She raised her hand again, and the bidding war commenced.

As the price was pushed up and up by denominations of fifty, Lacey glanced around the room, trying to find the bidder she was battling against. Her gaze fell on Colin.

When recognition sparked in his eyes, he held up an apologetic hand to her.

"Seven hundred and fifty pounds," the auctioneer said, looking at Colin. Colin graciously bowed out of the sale with a shake of the head.

The auctioneer looked back at Lacey. "We have two David Alfaro Siqueiros paintings going for seven hundred pounds. Seven hundred pounds. Can I get seven fifty? Seven fifty? Seven twenty-five? Seven ten?" He looked around the hall before his gaze fell back on Lacey. "Sold for seven hundred pounds!"

The gavel came down, sealing the deal, and a grin spread across Lacey's lips.

When five minutes had elapsed, Lacey left her seat and headed to the main office to pay and collect her paintings. She was the first person inside, and there was no one yet manning the counters. Chester paced back and forth seemingly as impatient as she was, then tipped his head up at the sound of the door they'd entered through opening. He started wagging his tail.

Curious, Lacey turned. It was Colin.

"Fancy bumping into you here," he joked as Chester trotted up to him like they were old friends.

Lacey felt a smile tug at the corners of her mouth. "Colin. Did you just make a purchase?"

"I did. An oil painting. Not quite in the same caliber of David Alfaro Siqueiros." A knowing smile appeared on his lips. "Sorry for pushing up the price of them. I didn't realize you were the other bidder."

"No need to apologize," Lacey told him. "I still got them for a steal. And it was kind of you to let me win after I completely failed to save you a seat."

Colin laughed. "What can I say? I was raised to be a gentleman."

He grinned his angelic smile, and Lacey felt her cheeks warm. The conversation was distinctly flirty, and while it was nice to get some attention from a handsome man, she would never do anything to jeopardize her relationship with Tom. Besides, she still had to find one of the Sawyer sons to speak to about her father, and she was letting herself get distracted. Again.

At last, a smartly dressed woman came from the back room up to the counter. "Sorry to keep you waiting," she said, beckoning Lacey over.

Lacey went up to pay for and collect her paintings. She guessed that the woman at the counter was not one of the Sawyer sons—being a woman and all—but perhaps if she'd worked here for a while she might have a recollection of Lacey's father.

Lacey just about got the guts up to ask when a second woman came from the back room to the counter and gestured for Colin to approach. He sidled up next to Lacey, casually leaning his elbow on the counter. Lacey shut her mouth again. The moment was lost.

"So, what's on your agenda for the rest of the day?" Colin asked Lacey, as the woman at his counter went to fetch his artwork.

"Chester and I have an afternoon of treasure hunting," Lacey told him. "Then we're heading back to my store."

"You own a store?" Colin asked, sounding impressed. "Let me guess … if you're buying the Siqueiros paintings for decoration then it must be something classy. Furniture?"

"Close," Lacey replied. "Actually, the paintings aren't for decoration. I'm selling them on. I'm an antiquer and auctioneer."

"Are you really?" Colin said, his eyebrows raising. "How fascinating."

The woman at the counter looked up from the till, her gaze flicking from Colin to Lacey with intrigue. Lacey immediately understood why. Colin was flirting.

Feeling a blush creep into her cheeks, Lacey realized she had to nip this in the bud before it got awkward.

"That's all gone through," the woman said, handing Lacey's credit card back to her. "Here's your receipt. And your paintings, wrapped and ready to go."

Lacey thanked her and quickly tucked a painting under each arm before she turned to Colin.

"It was nice to meet you," she said quickly while he was distracted with his own payment, and hurried away before he had a chance to suggest coffee or lunch or anything similar.

Out in the foyer, Lacey took a breath, only to discover she'd scurried away so fast, she'd left Chester behind! She couldn't go back in for him now. It would give off the wrong impression.

Luckily, at that moment, Chester came bounding out into the foyer. He looked thoroughly displeased at having been left behind.

"There you are," Lacey said, as she hurried out of the auction house at a clip, Chester at her heels.

Lacey trotted down the steps and marched to the van. She carefully added the paintings to the rest of her merchandise in the back seats, then jumped up into the driver's seat and looked over at Chester.

"I know what you're thinking," she said.

He blinked.

"I completely failed to speak to anyone about my dad. I just lost my nerve. And Colin kept distracting me."

She didn't want to go back in now. It would be asking for trouble!

"I have their number on the flyer," she continued, reeling out yet more excuses to Chester. "I'll call them once I'm home, I promise. That would be better anyway if you think about it. It will give me time to mentally prepare."

Chester gave her a suspicious eyebrow twitch. He clearly wasn't buying it, and Lacey wasn't surprised; she wasn't buying her excuses either. But her fear of knowing the previously unknown was too great. For today, at least, her search for her father would be put on the back burner.

# CHAPTER SIX

Lacey's next stop on her tour was the art store in Weymouth. She was particularly excited for this stop; she'd gotten quite into oil paintings during her decorating spree at Crag Cottage and was eager to see whether she could find some hidden gems. But before she had a chance to set off from the parking lot of Sawyer & Sons, her stomach grumbled loudly.

Lacey realized she hadn't eaten enough today. Considering how many wonderful different dishes she'd seen on sale, it was a sin not to have tried any of them!

She checked her phone app to see if there were any good places to stop for food on the way to Weymouth. Disappointingly, the only close option was a convenience store in a gas station.

"Chips and sandwiches for lunch?" Lacey said to Chester, looking on the bright side. "I'll use it as an excuse to try some weird British snacks."

Tom was always talking Lacey out of trying British junk food by reminding her she wasn't exactly missing anything while tempting her away by wafting the scent of one of his signature baked pastries toward her.

Thinking of Tom made Lacey's chest sink. She pushed the thoughts away and started the van. As she maneuvered out of the parking lot of the auction house, she spotted Colin in her rearview mirror, trotting down the steps. She hit the gas and sped away.

It was a bright day, and the tree-lined country lanes looked stunning in the sunshine. Lacey traversed hills and fields before she found the pokey little gas station beside a very traditional-looking British pub called The Red Lion. She filled up Tom's tank with gas (it was only polite to return it with a full tank, after all), then went into the store and perused the shelves of brightly packaged snack foods. She chose a box of Jaffa Cakes (which, by the picture on the front, appeared to be round spongy cakes with an orange jelly filling and chocolate coating), a packet of pickled onion–flavored chips (which were clearly targeted at children by the looks of the lurid purple packaging covered in cartoon monsters), and a generic ham sandwich from the cooler.

At the till, she grabbed Chester a chewy dog treat. Then she took her nutritionally lacking picnic back to the van and started munching away behind the steering wheel as she drove through the winding country lanes to the last destination on her treasure hunt.

Chester stretched out in the back seat of the van noisily working his way through his bone-shaped treat.

"I'll give that sandwich five out of ten," she told him in the rearview mirror. "The bread was a bit soggy. And the ham was kind of tasteless. And there was nowhere near enough condiments." She paused. "On second thought, I'll give it a four."

She'd been very spoiled by Tom's home-baked loaves, Lacey realized now, and the organic honey-glazed ham he always got from the farmer's market.

"Now ... let's try this Monster Munch."

She opened the pack and the stench of onions wafted out. Cautiously, Lacey took out one of the monster-feet-shaped chips and popped it in her mouth.

She regretted it immediately. The flavor was intense, a tangy sharpness that seemed to ignite taste buds that had thus far remained dormant her entire thirty-nine years.

Her eyes watered. She abandoned the packet on the passenger seat.

"That's meant for kids?" she exclaimed.

So Tom was right. She wasn't missing out on anything with regards to British snack foods.

Just then, Lacey saw a road sign for Weymouth and turned into the picturesque little town. It ran alongside a river, and there were cottages and tree-lined streets in full bloom.

The small art store was in the annex of a church building—a yellow brick new build with a block glass crucifix-shaped window. The cherry trees in the yard outside were shedding their pink and white blossoms like snow.

Lacey parked beside the curb, then entered in through the large glass doors.

Inside the art store, the space was vast and bright, with big windows and skylights letting in plenty of summer sunshine, and a cool breeze from the air conditioning making it feel airy. The walls were a stark white, the floorboards pale, varnished beech, and it was so serene, Lacey felt like she ought to be quiet. She gestured for Chester to be quiet with a finger to the lips. He tipped his head in acknowledgment, but his claws still clicked on the boards as he followed Lacey as she tiptoed across the room toward the displays.

Lacey perused the prints searching for horse-related ones. There were many reproductions of famous paintings by Edgar Degas and George Stubbs, but from what Gina had told her, the horse festival attendees weren't the sort of people to hang reprints on their walls. They would want originals.

Lacey was about to head toward the counter to speak to the clerk but was distracted by a beautiful hanging tapestry. It was a gorgeous appliqué in red and gold, and though it wasn't suitable for her upcoming auction, it would be perfect for the large empty space beside the big window on the second-floor landing of Crag Cottage.

Just then, Lacey felt Chester nudging his nose into her palm.

"I know," she murmured. "I'm not supposed to be shopping for myself. But just look at it. It's gorgeous."

Chester let out a whine of exasperation.

"Do you need any help?" a male voice said from behind Lacey.

She swirled on the spot to find the store clerk standing behind her. He was a portly man, short and stocky, with a kind face lined with wrinkles.

"I was just admiring this beautiful tapestry," Lacey told him.

The man flashed her a coy smile. "Thank you, I don't get many compliments on my appliqués."

"You made it?" Lacey exclaimed, surprised.

"I did," he said.

He seemed very humble, Lacey thought. Almost embarrassed by his exceptional talent.

"There's not much of a market for tapestries," he continued, wistfully. "Or original paintings, unfortunately. Most people are only after prints by famous painters."

Lacey exchanged a look with Chester. How could she resist now, after hearing the man's woeful story?

Chester's eyebrows twitched as if with defeat.

"Well, I guess in that case I'm not most people," Lacey told the clerk. "I'll take it."

His eyes lit up. "Really? You will?"

She nodded. "I will. And I'd very much like to see what other originals you have for sale."

The man looked thrilled. "Of course. Right this way."

He gestured with his arm and Lacey followed him as he bustled through an archway into the next room. Here it was even more like a museum or gallery, because the walls were adorned with paintings displayed side by side.

Lacey immediately homed in on an oil painting, a landscape of spring trees beside a river, with grazing horses in the foreground. It was exactly the sort of thing she was looking for. She paced over and read the signature: John Mace. She recognized the name. He was a popular British artist, and this was just the sort of piece she wanted to sell at her auction.

"I'll take this one," she told the clerk, excitement rippling through her.

The clerk hurried over and stuck a little red sticker next to it. Lacey moved on to the next painting that had caught her eye.

It was a watercolor by Mabel Gear, an artist from the 1950s whose paintings were frequently reproduced for greetings cards, and it was displayed next to an equally great find—a graphite master sketch of horses by the French artist Alexandre Pau De Saint Martin, dated 1800.

"I'll take both of these, too," Lacey said.

"You like horses," the clerk commented, excitedly placing his little red stickers next to the two artworks.

"Actually, my customers do," she told him. "I'm an auctioneer. I'm holding an auction for the Summer Equestrian Festival in Wilfordshire."

The clerk's eyes widened with recognition. "Why didn't you say? I have just the thing!"

He hurried over to a door at the side of the room, pulling a bunch of keys from his pocket as he went. He unlocked the door with one hand, beckoning for Lacey to follow with the other. Curious, Lacey walked over.

As the clerk opened the door, a sort of storeroom-cum-artist's studio was revealed. It was filled with industrial shelves and sawdust. Two grimy skylights above lit up a loom and a big workbench table covered in blocks of wood and sanding equipment.

"Now, where did I put it?" the clerk said as he started scanning the shelves. "Aha! Here."

He moved aside to reveal a bronze sculpture of a jockey.

Lacey's mouth fell open. She recognized it immediately. It was an Isidore Bonheur, one of the nineteenth century's most distinguished French animalier sculptors, whose cast bronze sculptures were sought-after antiques. A statue in good condition could fetch thousands of pounds at auction.

"May I take a closer look?" Lacey asked, feeling little trembles of excitement in her hands.

"Of course," the clerk said. "I keep it out back because no one seems interested in it."

"I'm interested," Lacey murmured.

She inspected the sculpture. It depicted a triumphant jockey patting the flank of its horse, made of bronze and set on a marble plinth. It was one of the artist's most popular designs, a commercial success he'd had cast in four different sizes, if she recalled correctly, and was in excellent condition, with next to no scratches or marks. It was a stunning and magnificent find that left Lacey nearly breathless.

That was, until she saw the price tag. Two thousand pounds.

Lacey balked. It was a lot of money to put down all in one go on one item. Lacey had learned a hard lesson about putting down too much money on stock during her time renovating the Lodge with Suzy. That had almost ended in financial ruin for her. And if she bought the sculpture, it would drain every last penny of her profit from the Roman coin.

"I can see you're deliberating," the clerk said. "Let me leave you with your thoughts for a moment while I attend to this customer."

Lacey had been so enthralled by the sculpture she'd not even heard the door open, nor the sound of heavy footsteps of another customer as he paced around perusing the artworks.

"Of course," she said. "Thank you."

The clerk headed off into the other room, leaving Lacey to mull over her options.

The sculpture was an amazing find. It would certainly cause some hype for her auction. Indeed, it may well even be THE big-ticket item with which to lure people in. Whether she was able to recoup her investment would really come down to her skill on auction day. As long as she didn't choke, and worked the crowd properly, it could mean a big win for her. But a big win was also a big risk. Her normal method was to have a range of diverse, unique, and good quality merchandise, splurge items the average person could still afford if they felt like treating themselves. But this sculpture could only be sold to the customers attending the festival. If no one bought it during her auction, then she'd have to wait a whole year until they came back. Keeping a load of expensive stock unsold for a year was far from ideal.

As Lacey weighed her options, she could hear the murmuring voices of the clerk and his customer in the other room. There was something familiar about the customer's voice, and Lacey was hit by a hunch.

"Wait a second … " she muttered as she paced over to the door and peeked out.

She was right. It was Colin!

# CHAPTER SEVEN

W hat was he doing here? Lacey thought. Had he followed her? How else would he have arrived in Weymouth, in the same obscure art store in the annex of a church, down a quiet cherry tree–lined road?

She hadn't noticed him driving behind her at any point, but that didn't mean he hadn't; she'd been so preoccupied with soggy sandwiches and beautiful countryside she could have easily missed him tailing her. The thought of it made her shudder.

Chester barked excitedly at the sight of the familiar face, completely blowing her cover. His claws click-clacked on the floorboards as he trotted over to greet Colin.

Colin glanced up. "Well, if it isn't Chester!" he said, ruffling the dog's ears. Then his gaze flicked over to where Lacey was half hiding behind the wall, and his eyes sparked with amusement. "Lacey. Fancy catching you here."

Lacey stepped from around the wall and folded her arms, adopting a guarded, suspicious pose. "What are you doing here?"

Colin didn't look fazed by her less than cordial tone. "I heard from someone at Sawyer's that there was an Isidore Bonheur sculpture for sale here. I came to check it out."

The clerk piped up. "I was just telling the gentleman that you already have first dibs. But it seems as if you already know each other?"

"We're old friends," Colin quipped. "We go way back."

"We're barely acquaintances," Lacey amended. She looked away from Colin and back to the clerk. "I've made my decision. I'm going to take the statue."

The clerk's eyebrows rose with surprise. Chester tipped his head to the side and let out a noise of confusion.

Lacey knew she was being rash, but something about Colin's presence made her want to leave as soon as possible. She didn't trust him. It felt to her like he was up to something.

"Brilliant," the clerk said, seemingly oblivious to the atmosphere. "I'll get packing!"

He hurried off with a triumphant look, leaving Lacey alone with Colin.

"You beat me to it," Colin said, flashing her a genial smile. "Again."

He was behaving just as warmly as he had at the auction house, but Lacey couldn't quell her suspicions.

"I guess today's not your day," she said, a little stiffly. "So tell me, where is it you're heading next? We seem to be on the same treasure hunt."

She figured if she knew where he was going next, then if he turned up at the same place as her she'd know he was following her. She'd be able to catch him in a trick, if he was indeed playing one.

"Why? Did you want to come with me?" He wiggled his eyebrows.

Lacey tightened her folded arms. "No. I'm just curious."

A knowing smirk spread across his lips. "You know what they say about curiosity. It killed the cat."

Lacey flared her nostrils. "Good thing I'm not a cat then," she replied in a deadpan tone.

The clerk bustled into the room then, his jolliness shifting the energy in the room. Under his arm, Lacey caught sight of a bulky item wrapped in bubble wrap. The Isidore Bonheur.

A tightness starting to form in her throat. Was she being crazy putting down such a huge amount on one item? It would wipe out all her profits from the coin. And if she wasn't able to sell it at the auction, would she end up hanging on to it for years with no interested parties, like the art store owner had?

Then she remembered a little pearl of wisdom Naomi had told her from her yoga retreat year. Physiologically, nerves and excitement are the same thing. She just had to channel her nerves at taking such a huge risk into excitement, and use that excitement to power her through to her goal.

Which was easier said than done, because the clerk was ringing up all her purchases at the till, and the figure on the digital screen was climbing higher and higher.

Her pulse started thrumming in her ears.

*I'm not nervous, I'm excited* ... . she tried to tell herself. *I'll make the money back at the auction.*

At least, she *should* make the money back at the auction. But there were no guarantees in the world of auctioneering. It was hard enough to predict the outcome for a normal auction, let alone a special one with a new and unfamiliar clientele. The horsey people were an unknown entity to Lacey, and she really had no idea what to expect from them. According to Gina, their favorite hobby was parting with their cash, but whether they decided to do so at her auction house, and on her wares, was a different matter altogether.

The till bleeped as the clerk punched in the final item—the tapestry for the wall of Crag Cottage—and the digital display updated itself. Lacey's mouth went as dry as the Sahara. Parting with this kind of money was nothing for the Saskias of the world, but Lacey wasn't used to being well off yet, and it still felt a little alarming for her. Especially considering the tapestry wasn't for the auction at all, and she'd just splurged on it in a moment of bravado.

*It's one of a kind,* she told herself. *It will pay you back in joy.*

"Are you okay?" Colin asked from beside her, his tone hinting at amusement. "You've gone quite pale."

"I'm fine," Lacey replied, tersely. She handed her credit card to the clerk.

"Are you going to be able to carry all that?" the clerk asked, looking at all the neat parcels he'd wrapped for her.

"I can help," Colin offered.

"No thank you," Lacey said.

"Are you sure?" Colin pressed.

"Quite sure," Lacey said, awkwardly attempting to find a way to hold all the packages in one go, and failing spectacularly.

"Come on," Colin insisted. "That's no way to treat precious antiques."

The clerk handed Lacey back her card, and it proved to be the straw that broke the camel's back. The bubble-wrapped statue slipped from beneath Lacey's armpits.

She gasped as she watched the rare antique plummet toward the countertop, before it was caught, barely an inch from making contact, by Colin.

"Okay," Lacey said, haughtily, trying to save face. "I suppose an extra pair of hands would be useful."

She thanked the clerk, then headed for the exit, leaving Chester and Colin to catch up as she crossed the road, her cheeks hot with embarrassment, and unlocked the van.

"A van-driving antiquarian," Colin commented, as she busied herself packing the new items safely away in the back. "You are quite the puzzle."

Lacey said nothing. Colin peered in through the passenger side window, at the empty sandwich package lying on the seat, next to the pickled onion chips and Jaffa cakes.

"You eat junk food from convenience stores?" he teased. "Curiouser and curiouser."

Lacey knew the quote well. It was from *Alice in Wonderland*, one of her favorite novels.

She peered over her shoulder at Colin, still not sure what to make of him. Him turning up in Weymouth seemed highly suspect to her. But what exactly she had to be suspicious about, she couldn't be sure. He was like a moth to a flame. Was the flame her?

"Let's get tea," he said, boldly. "Your lunch was pitiful."

Lacey was taken aback. She shook her head and stammered, "I can't. I need to get back to Wilfordshire. My store's really busy at the moment. I only have one employee. She's already mad at me."

"But by the time you get back, won't it already be past closing time?" He smiled angelically.

Lacey checked her watch. He was right. She'd spent far longer treasure hunting than she'd expected. There was no way she'd make it back in time to catch Gina now.

"What do you say?" Colin pressed. "I know a great cafe that makes Dorset apple traybake. It's just round the corner."

Lacey *was* hungry. Her lunch had been disappointing and extremely unfulfilling. And after all the amazing street foods she'd seen on sale today it did seem a shame that the only thing she'd sampled was a vegan muffin.

And anyway, it wasn't like there was anyone else she was supposed to be spending the evening with...

"I suppose I do owe you a coffee," Lacey said, finally.

"Great! It's this way."

Lacey followed Colin along the pretty street, wondering if she'd just made a very bad decision.

# Chapter Eight

"I'll take a slice of Dorset apple traybake and a macchiato," Lacey said to the waitress standing next to the table where she and Colin were sitting (a genuine turn-of-the-century Persian marble top bistro table, Lacey noted with admiration).

"I'll have the same," Colin replied.

The waitress left, and Colin let out a cheerful guffaw.

"What's so funny?" Lacey queried.

"You. Checking out the furniture."

"It's antique," Lacey replied. "These can sell for up to a thousand pounds if they're kept in good condition."

Colin smirked. "And the chairs?"

"Alfresco wicker," Lacey told him with a nonchalant shrug. "Sixty if you're lucky."

He laughed again. "You're quite the expert." There was a glint of admiration in his eye. "You said you're an auctioneer as well?"

"That's right. I'm holding an auction this weekend. I was on a stock run when we met."

"I see," Colin said, sounding intrigued.

Just then, the waitress returned with their coffees and cakes. The conversation ceased as she placed them gently onto the table. Lacey licked her lips at the delicious-looking cake, a buttercup-yellow sponge with thin slices of apples layered on top and dusted with white icing powder.

"Bon appétit," Colin said.

Lacey forked some of the apple cake into her mouth. She hadn't been expecting it to be warm, but this one had that straight-out-of-the-oven warmth to it. The sponge was delightfully moist, with just enough spiced cinnamon to complement the sweetness of the apples.

"Wow, this is so tasty," Lacey said.

She'd have to tell Tom about it. It was exactly the sort of thing he loved.

"It's a favorite of mine," Colin said. "Reminds me of being a child. My mother and I used to bake it together."

Lacey noted the mournful look in his eyes, and guessed his mother had passed. She felt a surge of gratitude for her own mother, Shirley, even though they butted heads at the best of times.

"Did you grow up around here?" Lacey asked.

Colin nodded. "Bridport. It's a little market town on the coast."

"Sounds like Wilfordshire," Lacey said.

"And where did you grow up?" Colin asked. "My bet is you're not local."

"Gee, what gave it away?" Lacey joked, in her best Scarlett O'Hara accent. "You guessed it. I grew up in New York."

"How fantastic. And are you married? I don't see a ring."

Lacey almost choked on her macchiato. Colin was forthcoming, and it took her by surprise.

"Divorced," she said. "Earlier this year. Best decision I ever made."

"I'm divorced too. Also a good decision. My only regret is how hard it was on the kids."

"Luckily I don't have any of those," Lacey said, thinking again about her auburn-haired nephew back in New York City. There may not have been any children of her own to harm during her divorce, but leaving home had meant leaving Frankie, and she missed him.

"Do you want them?"

Lacey shrugged. "That's the million-dollar question. I never did. It's why David and I separated."

"And now?"

"And now I'm warming up to the idea. But I'm going to be forty in a few days, and I don't want to change my mind only to find out it's too late."

Colin gave her a sympathetic nod, and Lacey wondered why she'd found herself being so open to this stranger. She'd opened up to him about things she'd not yet discussed with Tom. Perhaps just because he was a stranger, it made it easier. Perhaps it was because Tom was always so busy and so focused on pastries that it never seemed appropriate to bring it up.

Whatever the reason, Lacey was glad to have had a chance to air her concerns to a sympathetic ear. Any suspicion she had over Colin disappeared. He was just a charming man, with a kind smile, and an excellent taste in dessert.

She took another bite of Dorset apple traybake.

"I'd take this over a Jaffa Cake any day," she murmured.

It was dark by the time Lacey made it back to Wilfordshire. Her day trip had ended up being vastly different than what she'd expected. She'd found a compelling lead to pursue regarding her father and had enjoyed the company of a handsome, smooth-talking man. The whole thing had left her feeling quite discombobulated.

Despite the fatigue settling over her, Lacey still had one more task to complete before she could return to Crag Cottage and retire to bed, and that was to lock all of her treasures safely away in the store.

She took the promenade route toward the high street, noting how much busier it seemed than was usual for this time of the evening. In fact, it was almost as busy as Bournemouth beach had been during peak hour.

Surveying the scene, Lacey saw well-dressed couples, groups of men and women, and some fresh-faced college-age youths milling around the street. They all had the same look about them, the sort of confident put-togetherness that came with wealth. Lacey realized they were the rich horsey people Gina had told her about. They must have been arriving throughout the day while she'd been away, probably to settle in over the weekend in advance of the festival's kick-off. But their sudden presence made Lacey feel even more peculiar, as if her life as she'd known it had become irrevocably changed.

Lacey tried to put her existential ruminations out of her mind—it was a bad habit she fell into sometimes when she was overtired—and turned the van onto the high street. But here, it was even more crowded! The Coach House Inn on the corner was completely surrounded by revelers. She'd seen pubs in London like that, where the streets were overtaken by patrons with next to no regard for the rules of the road, but she'd never expected to see such a thing in Wilfordshire! There were so many people standing on the cobblestone streets, it may as well have been officially pedestrianized.

Lacey had no choice but to slow to a crawl and inch the van slowly past the inebriated revelers, taking painstaking care not to squish anyone's toes in the process. As she went, she saw more than one person quaffing champagne straight out of the bottle. Since the pub didn't normally sell champagne of that caliber, Lacey realized they must have stocked it specifically for this purpose. Gina was right. The horsey people were rich, and the businesses of Wilfordshire were going to profit from them enormously. Assuming the cost of cleaning up after them wasn't excessive ...

After a long crawl along the high street, Lacey finally made it to her store and parked against the curb. She was relieved to see that Gina had properly secured the store, having lowered and locked the steel security shutters into place. With all these strangers milling about the place, Lacey couldn't be too careful. There may well be opportunists lurking among the crowds.

Lacey twisted her key to operate the mechanism and raise the metal shutters. They rattled slowly and noisily upward, revealing the glass windows inch by inch. As the shutters cleared eye height, Lacey got her first glimpse of Gina's poster, which she'd stuck inside the window.

Instead of a so-called "retired racing horse" being in the center of the otherwise quite tastefully designed poster, there was a sad, scragglylooking donkey.

"Gina!" Lacey exclaimed.

But she was too tired to care about the mix-up, really. It was one way to get noticed, she figured.

She headed inside and began unloading all of her amazing purchases into the back storeroom, excited all over again by the hoard she'd amassed. Then she parked Tom's van on the side street beside the patisserie and switched into her Volvo.

Once home, she headed straight to bed. It had been quite the day. And while she'd thoroughly enjoyed her innocent lunch with Colin, she couldn't help but wonder whether Tom would see the liaison quite as innocently as she did.

# Chapter Nine

L acey woke to a suffocatingly stuffy room. Before even checking the time, she leapt out of bed and pushed open the French doors that led to the balcony for some fresh air.

As the hot ocean wind gusted into her bedroom, she looked out over the cliffs and down to the beach. To her surprise, her usually quiet corner of the beach was full of people. And not just the usual dog walkers and joggers who might venture this far on a warm summer's morning, either. It was full of sunbathers, swimmers, and picnickers. By the looks of the smoldering remains of bonfires and disposable barbeques, some of the revelers were still going from the night before.

Astonished, Lacey leaned over the railing to get a better view toward town. The closer to the epicenter she peered, the more people she saw, all packed in like sardines, making Wilfordshire's beach look as crowded as Bournemouth's. Her little town had been transformed, and Lacey felt a surge of excitement to get to her shop and see what the day had in store for her.

She headed back inside to get ready. As she did so, she noticed the Sawyer & Sons pamphlet lying on her bedside table, where she'd left it the night before. The auction house might just hold the final puzzle piece she was looking for in the search for her missing father. She'd promised herself she'd call them once she was home.

She paced over and picked the pamphlet up, gazing at the telephone number she needed to dial. Just one call might change everything. But she couldn't bring herself to do it. She'd barely digested her emotions about what she'd learned during her day trip.

Instead, she opened the top drawer of her dresser and put the pamphlet away inside. Out of sight, out of mind. For the time being. At least until the festival was over, anyway.

Lacey turned to continue her morning routine, only to discover Chester sitting at the end of the bed, watching her with what could only be described as an expression of disapproval.

"There are just too many other things I need to do first," Lacey told him, trying to justify her continued postponements.

Chester whined his disappointment. Lacey ignored his pointed glare as she went into the en suite to shower.

Once she was clean, she dressed and piled her wet hair into a loose bun, then trotted down to the kitchen, knocked back an espresso, and slid on her shoes.

"Come on, boy," she called to Chester. "Time to vamoose."

He bolted out the barn-style back door and streaked across the lawn toward Gina's sheep, sending them running. Lacey followed after him, taking the path he'd cleared for her through the herd, and knocked a jaunty rhythm on her best friend's back door with her knuckles.

Coming from inside, she heard the scraping sound of the bolt being drawn across, then the top hatch swung open and a disheveled-looking Gina blinked at her from the other side.

"Yikes," Lacey said. "Is everything okay? You look a little worse for wear."

"Charming," Gina replied. She paced back into her kitchen and began filling her backpack with provisions for the busy workday ahead. "I just didn't get much sleep."

Lacey remembered all the rich tourists she'd seen partying in the town last night, and thought of all the revelers still going on the beach this morning.

"Were you out with the horsey people last night?" she queried.

Gina yawned. "If you can't beat them, you join them."

Lacey giggled at the mental picture that formed in her mind, of Gina in her red glasses and Wellington boots in the moonlit streets of

Wilfordshire, a champagne bottle wielded above her head, can-can dancing with the rich horsey folk.

Boudica padded into the kitchen, looking just as sleepy as her mother.
But the moment she saw Chester, she went running for the door, shoved
the bottom part open with her nose, and wrestled him to the ground in a
sweetly ferocious play-fight.

"So, did you meet any eligible bachelors?" Lacey asked, as Gina slid
on her wellies.

"Maybe," Gina said mischievously.

Lacey's eyes widened. "Gina? Do you have a *man* in there?"

"Now you're being ridiculous," Gina said. She took Boudica's leash
off the hook by the door. "You know I'd never take someone home on a
first date." She smirked.

"So there was a date?" Lacey squealed, grasping her friend by the
arm and practically yanking her out the door. "Tell me everything!"

They headed across the lawn and down the cliff path together, pups
in tow.

"He's Swiss," Gina explained as they went. "I met him in the Coach
House. The horsey folk completely take it over for the whole week.
Goodness knows when they actually watch any of the official events, it
seems like they're in there from dawn until dusk!"

They reached the busy beach. Boudica and Chester spotted a cluster
of new dogs all trying to catch the same ball, and pelted across the sand
to sniff out any potential new friends.

Gina and Lacey began their brisk walk along the coastline.

"When you get married in Zurich, can I be the bridesmaid?" Lacey
teased.

"It won't come to that," Gina said, with a shake of the head. "Mr. Rich
is only here for the week and then he'll go again. To be perfectly honest,
that's just how I like it. One week of male attention is plenty to sustain
me for the rest of the year!"

At her mention of male attention, Lacey thought of Colin. Their
afternoon coffee chat had been pleasant, and Colin had come around in
her mind from a slightly creepy pursuer to a somewhat charming gentleman. And therein lay the problem.

She bit down on her lip. "I think I accidentally flirted with a man yesterday," she confessed.

"Oh?" Gina replied.

"I met him at the auction house. He has a Border collie like Chester, so we started talking about that. Then we bumped into one another again in an art store." She paused, still not one hundred percent certain their meeting in the art store had been by chance. "We were after the same antique, but I beat him to it. When I realized I wasn't going to make it home in time to help you close up the store, I agreed to go for coffee and cake with him."

Gina narrowed her eyes contemplatively. "Who paid?"

"It was a fifty-fifty split."

"Good. That sets a tone of friendship rather than romance."

"It does?" Having spent well over a decade as a married woman, Lacey had completely forgotten what the rules were.

"Yes," Gina said, deadly seriously. "And did you talk about Tom?"

Lacey racked her brain. She hadn't. She'd not even mentioned him. And added to that she'd talked about her divorce, probably inadvertently giving off the impression she was free and single.

"No," she confessed meekly.

"Oh, Lacey," came Gina's reproachful response. "That's not a good sign."

Lacey felt a flutter of panic in her chest. She'd not meant anything by it, she was just lonely and Colin seemed like a friendly guy with whom she had a lot in common to talk about. But she could see how it might seem from an outsider's perspective.

"It wasn't like I was avoiding talking about him," Lacey tried to explain.

"But you did. Unconsciously," Gina replied. "Which meant you were willfully flirting."

"Willfully flirting?" Lacey echoed. "You make it sound like a crime. I love Tom. I'd never do anything to hurt him. Do you think I should tell him about it?"

"I think that would be for the best," her confidante replied with a sympathetic smile.

Lacey nodded her agreement. "If only I could pin him down for five seconds to do it," she added.

"Good point," Gina replied. "He's going to be far too busy today for a social call. As will we." She gestured to all the people on the beach to illustrate her point. There really were a lot of them!

"It was busy yesterday, I take it?" Lacey asked.

"It was," Gina replied. "We're going to need to do some restocking this morning. It's looking rather bare."

"That's a good idea," Lacey said. "We don't want a half-empty store. It'll make us look like a pair of asses."

Gina squinted her eyes. "I take it you saw the poster."

"Yes, I saw the poster! A donkey? Gina, I think you need new glasses."

"I told you, it was so busy. I must've clicked on the wrong picture and emailed it to the printers without double checking. Goodness knows why they didn't think to ask me if I really want an ass on my poster for a horse show, but there you go."

Lacey started chuckling. "At least it's just one poster. I'm sure it will give the locals a good giggle."

"About that..." Gina said.

Lacey looked over at her. "What now?"

"The printers sort of talked me into a promotional deal. I got enough for the high street."

Lacey sighed. "Don't you remember me saying to get *one* poster? And how many did you buy? Fifteen? Twenty?"

"Fifty."

Lacey couldn't help it. She burst out laughing. Only Gina could make a little mistake fifty times worse.

"They were very persuasive!" Gina said defensively.

The two women veered off the beach and onto the promenade. They reached their favorite coffee shop, where a queue was stretching right out the door.

"I haven't had to get in line for coffee since my New York days," Lacey commented.

"Didn't you hear?" Gina said. "Wilfordshire's the hip new place to be these days. Or at least for the next week."

They took their place at the back of the queue, behind a smartly dressed middle-aged couple. Gina nudged Lacey, pointed at their backs, and mouthed, "Rich horsey people!"

Lacey nodded her agreement. It was obvious just from their clothes they were out-of-towners. None of the women in Wilfordshire would wear stilettos at breakfast, and the men wore their shirts tucked into jeans, not suit pants. Added to that, the woman was complaining about the uneven cobblestones hurting her feet (hence the unspoken *no stilettos before breakfast rule,* Lacey thought) and the man was complaining that he was too hot because there wasn't enough shade in the town (*so why not take off your waistcoat?*).

The queue took ages to go down, forcing Lacey and Gina to endure the couple's constant whining, but finally they were served and left with their coffees. As they headed up the high street, Lacey noticed that a lot of the stores seemed to have jacked up their prices from yesterday. Jane's toy store, which usually sold wooden kids toys, now had a row of beautiful, handcrafted rocking horses lined up outside with very big price tags to match. The shoe shop now seemed to entirely stock leather riding boots, and Taryn's boutique mannequins were dressed in jockey-inspired couture.

As Lacey waited for the shutters to rise, she glanced over at Tom's patisserie. He'd opened early to catch the breakfast crowd, and it was already packed inside.

"Looks like he was inspired by our donkey," Gina said, pointing at the macaron display.

Tom clearly hadn't found enough time to fix his macaron horse properly. The head he'd made to replace the last one was made with lavender macarons, which looked gray from where they were standing. It was also too big for the body, and to put it bluntly, was quite ugly. Not that it had put off the customers.

Lacey laughed, then laughed again when she turned back to the store window, the shutters now rolled all the way up, and saw the donkey poster on proud display. "We should probably take that down."

"Absolutely not," Gina said. "It's charming. Besides, I was reading the website last night and you can actually donate to the horses and donkeys there. We could donate some of the proceeds from the auction to them. Then if anyone laughs about the poster, we can guilt trip them into donating too!"

Lacey gave her a peculiar look. "Your mind works in strange ways," she said, as she unlocked the front door. "I'll definitely make a donation, though. It's awful that some of the racehorses get abandoned when they're old."

She pushed the door open and entered the distinctly empty-looking store. She hadn't noticed in the darkness of yesterday evening, what with a head full of ruminations, but it had clearly been a very successful day.

"I see what you mean," Lacey said, surveying the bare shelves. "We've got a lot to do."

They immediately began carrying stock through from the backroom onto the main floor. The retro window display was looking particularly depleted.

"I didn't think they'd be the type to like lava lamps," Lacey said to Gina, as they maneuvered a paisley orange armchair into the gap that had been left.

"They seem to like anything that costs money," Gina commented.

"We'd better hurry," Lacey added, looking at the queues forming outside various stores on the street. "That bell's going to start tinkling off the hook soon enough."

She spoke too late. The door opened, the bell jangled, and in walked Mr. and Mrs. Rich Horsey. Or should that be Monsieur and Mademoiselle Cheval? The couple were French; the argument they were having with one another as they walked through the door immediately gave them away.

Lacey and Gina exchanged a glance. It was as if the couple didn't even care that they were there. They just kept on arguing, right in the middle of the store.

The woman went over to the crockery section and took down a plate. The man looked over his shoulder and found Gina and Lacey in the window.

"My wife wants this thing," he said brusquely. "God knows why. How much is it?"

Lacey steeled herself. She went over to the man and checked the ticket. "Forty pounds."

"How much is that in euros?" he asked, not even looking at her.

"I'm afraid I don't know," Lacey said.

"You don't know?" he spat, incredulously. "Why don't you know? Isn't it your job to know? All the other big stores put their prices in pounds *and* euros. Why don't you?"

"Because we're not a big store," Lacey told him simply. "We're a small independent, and we write all our labels by hand."

He rolled his eyes like this was the biggest inconvenience, then turned to his wife and spoke rapidly in French. By his hand gestures, Lacey deduced that he was telling her he wasn't going to buy the plate because he didn't know how much it cost. Then to Lacey's surprise, the woman began bawling, right in the middle of the store.

Eyebrows raised, Lacey looked over at Gina. Gina was quite clearly trying to stifle her laughter at the sight of a grown woman sobbing over a plate.

"Now look what you've done," the man barked at Lacey.

Lacey's capacity for speech completely failed her. Which was probably for the best, because her instinct was to ask how on earth his wife's childish tantrum was in any way her fault.

As Mademoiselle Cheval continued weeping, the main door opened with a tinkle and a woman in a purple velvet gown entered. But she took one look at the crying French woman before promptly turning around again and walking away.

Lacey had to get these two out of her store quick; they were driving away the customers!

She quickly made the conversion calculation in her head. "Forty pounds works out at about forty-three euros."

"Fine," the man said, slapping his credit card down on the counter. "Ring it up. She'll never stop otherwise."

"Great," Lacey said. "But I have to put it through in pounds, you understand."

"Yes, yes, whatever. Just hurry up."

Lacey bit her tongue to stifle her frustration. She went around behind the counter and rang up the sale. As soon as the wife realized what was happening, she stopped crying.

Lacey couldn't believe the behavior of these people. If the rest of the horsey people were like these two, she wasn't sure she'd be able to keep her cool.

She handed them their purchase and watched them leave before turning to Gina.

"Please don't tell me that's an indication of things to come," she said.

Gina flashed her a pitying smile. "I'm afraid that's just the tip of the iceberg."

"Great," Lacey muttered.

Her week ahead seemed suddenly intimidating. Had she bitten off more than she could chew when it came to the rich horsey folk?

# Chapter Ten

Lacey's muscles strained as she tugged the fold-out chairs through the storage room door. There was a lot she needed to get ready for the auction—from deciding the order of items she'd be selling, typing up the itinerary, and physically setting up the room—and time seemed to be in short supply.

"Lacey?" came Gina's voice from the shop floor. "How much is the Chinoiserie mantel clock? The red one with the pagoda roof?"

"Two hundred!" Lacey called back, before getting back to the task at hand.

"Will you take one fifty?" Gina called.

Lacey sighed and abandoned her task. This had been happening all day—her being interrupted mid-task by queries. But despite the busyness, she was still grateful for the custom.

She headed for the shop floor to deal with the situation herself. As worried as she was about how she'd find time to fit everything in before D-day, she still had a shop of customers to attend to. Or rather, a shop *stuffed full* of customers, she realized as she reached the main floor.

She shimmied her way through the browsers, finding Gina standing with an older gentleman who had bushy mutton-chop sideburns. His brown corduroy trousers and purple silk shirt immediately gave him away as one of the horsey people because only someone with no money worries could get away with dressing so eccentrically.

"Lacey can help you with your query," Gina said, gesturing to her with a hand.

The man turned to her. "Two hundred is a bit steep, don't you think?"

"Steep?" Lacey replied, jovially. "I think you mean a steal!" She took the clock from him, turning it around in her hands. It was a spectacular specimen, its peculiar design inspired by the architecture of pagodas, with a distinctive sakura flower pattern in red and gold. "I take a lot of pride in my mantel clocks, sir," she continued. "They're among my top selling items." She gestured to the busy shop floor. "And I've no need to drop the price, since I know someone else will be more than happy to pay for it in full."

The man smirked, one of his bushy eyebrows inching upward. "You drive a hard bargain," he said.

"I like to think I drive an honest one," Lacey said, meeting his expression with a cheeky grin.

He chuckled. "Fine. I'll take it! Two hundred it is."

Lacey felt triumphant. She pressed a hand to Gina's arm. "Could you ring this up for the gentleman?" she said, before flashing her a *that's-how-it's-done* look.

She was about to return to her chair-tugging task, when a familiar voice stopped her.

"I see you're holding another auction."

Lacey looked over. It was Taryn, her neighbor and nemesis.

For the first time ever, Taryn wasn't dressed all in black. Instead, she was wearing a silk, nip-waisted jacket in red over a ruffled white shirt, tight jeans, and high-heeled riding boots. She looked less like a walking corpse and more like a Victorian-era vampire. The only thing missing from the ensemble was a top hat and whip.

From her stern expression, Lacey guessed Taryn was here to complain about something. She braced herself.

"How can I help you, Taryn?" she asked, adopting the impassive, polite tone she always did when dealing with the petulant boutique owner from next door.

"I just want to remind you to keep the noise down during your auction," Taryn said. "You know our walls are paper thin, and the sound drives me and my customers nuts. All that rapid talking and banging. *'Sold!'*" she mimicked, using an offensively bad American accent. "You know these stores aren't meant for hundreds of people to sit in them for hours on end."

She would say that, Lacey thought. Her minimalist boutique only ever had a few customers inside it at any one time.

"I'll try my best," Lacey said, though she knew it would be impossible to meet Taryn's terms. Auctions were noisy by nature. "Anyway, I'm only expecting about a dozen participants, not hundreds."

Taryn pulled a face. "Don't be absurd. Your auction is just the sort of thing these horsey people love. You'll be over capacity, trust me. If there's anything to worry about, it'll be people getting annoyed for not being able to attend. Which reminds me, I'm not having my boutique entrance blocked by people queueing to get in, either. If my front door gets blocked for even a minute, I'll be forced to get the chain-link fences out of storage, and I'll charge you for the privilege."

"I'm sure it won't come to that," Lacey said, wondering what scenarios had presented themselves to Taryn in the past that she even owned steel crowd control fences.

"It better not," Taryn snapped. Then she turned and marched away.

Lacey watched her go, the cogs of her mind beginning to whirr. Was Taryn right? Would hundreds of people really want to come to her auction? Would there really be lines out the door?

Obviously, Taryn had a tendency for overexaggeration, but if she was correct on this occasion and there really were hundreds of people interested in Lacey's auction, where was she going to put them all?

Suddenly, a moment of inspiration struck Lacey. In her old job as an interior design assistant, she'd often attended auctions on behalf of Saskia. But of course her control-freak boss never let her bid on anything without checking with her first, so Lacey would end up having her on a conference call and relaying the proceedings to her like some kind of sports commentator. Saskia always said auction houses needed to modernize and set up some kind of live online interactive system. Well, what if Lacey did just that?

Feeling a surge of inspiration, Lacey thought it through. If attendees could watch the auction proceedings through a live feed, and have some kind of way to place their bids, then it would solve the problem of her not having enough space. Maybe once the system was in place and had been tried out this time, she could make her future auctions international, opening up her auction house to the whole world!

She was dreaming big, she knew that. But why not dream big? It was dreaming big that had brought her to Wilfordshire in the first place. Why couldn't she be the one to modernize the industry?

Lacey became more and more excited as her idea started to crystalize in her mind. She'd need someone tech savvy to help her, of course, since she was basically technologically incompetent. The app she shared with her mom and sister was really the most she could handle. It might not even be possible to set up an online system, especially in the short time frame, but perhaps someone more tech-literate than herself would be able to tell her how doable it really was. Gina, of course, would be no help. Tom had a more techy brain than Lacey did, but he was far too busy to ask.

"Suzy!" Lacey cried.

Her friend Suzy ran the Lodge B&B, and was her junior by seventeen years. Seventeen years made all the difference when it came to technological competence!

Itching with excitement, Lacey grabbed the old dial-up phone from the counter and punched in her friend's digits. But the call just rang and rang, before going unanswered.

*Now what?* Lacey thought. She really wanted to run with this idea before her self-saboteur talked her out of it. She could call the Lodge directly, of course, but her chances of actually getting hold of Suzy through the busy reception desk were slim to none. She'd stand more of a chance if she just turned up in person.

Lacey paused. There was still so much to do here, and so many customers in need of assistance. But if she didn't grab this moment now, she might never.

She snatched up her car keys and hurried around the counter, whistling to Chester.

He lifted his head, looking as excited as Lacey now felt about her online auction idea. He jumped to his feet and followed her as she beelined for the exit in an attempt to get away before anyone stopped her and asked any questions.

"Hey! Lacey?" Gina cried as she streaked past. "Where are you going?"

"Ummm … lunch break!" Lacey called back.

She hurried out the door before Gina could protest.

Out on the street, the effects of the Summer Equestrian Festival were becoming more and more evident. The streets looked like someone had blown up a fancy liquor store, with debris and bottles of expensive wine lying in the gutters. The poor street cleaners were working overtime to try and keep the town neat and tidy, but they were evidently losing the battle against the sheer number of festival attendees.

Lacey had never seen anything quite like it, outside of an actual music festival in a muddy field, that was. And she thought the English were meant to be genteel! Hadn't anyone told that to the drunk women in the fascinators dancing on the benches?

She reached her car and got inside, relieved for the sanctity. But her peace was short lived. When she turned on to the main road, she found it nearly impossible to actually drive. People were spilling over the sidewalks into the road, treating it like it was pedestrianized. Lacey realized her quick trip to the Lodge was going to take far longer than she'd anticipated. She'd definitely feel the wrath of Gina once she returned.

It was teatime when she reached the Lodge. She wasn't surprised to discover there was nowhere to park. The B&B must be fully booked for the festival. Lacey knew Suzy wouldn't mind her taking up a spot in the staff lot, so she drove around the back.

The staff lot was actually pretty busy too. Suzy must've hired more staff to deal with the extra work from the festival. Lacey spotted a couple of unfamiliar vehicles parked alongside Lucia's run-around and Suzy's four-by-four. A bright pink mini with fluffy pink dice caught her attention in particular.

She parked alongside it and cut the engine. Chester followed her out of the car.

As she headed in through the patio doors of the dining room, she was hit by a wall of noise. Every single chair at every single table was occupied by a designer-clothes-wearing, loud-talking person. The Lodge's wait staff were darting all over the place trying to appease their every whim.

"Darjeeling!" she heard a man shout. "What do you mean you don't have Darjeeling?"

The poor girl waiting at his table stammered, "We're all out."

"Then I'll have an Oolong."

"We don't sell Oolong," the girl said.

"No Oolong?" the man yelled. "This is preposterous! Next you'll be telling me you don't have Matcha!"

The intimidated girl shook her head. "Sorry, we don't."

Lacey couldn't just stand by and watch. She approached the table. "Sir, I know a wonderful tearoom on Wilfordshire's High Street," she said. "It's called Penny's. You won't be disappointed. Tell Penny that Lacey from the antiques store sent you and to put the tea on her tab."

The man regarded her suspiciously. Then he stood. "Fine. I will," he barked, before marching away. His seat was promptly taken by another man who'd been waiting.

The waitress flashed Lacey a look of gratitude, and Lacey headed off in search of Suzy.

The corridors of the Lodge were as equally busy and loud as the dining room, with people coming in and out of the drawing room and elevator. Lacey's head spun from the busyness of it all. She had no idea how Suzy was coping with everything.

"Lacey!" a voice squealed suddenly from behind.

Lacey swirled to find Suzy skipping toward her, beaming from ear to ear. Far from looking harried by the influx of tourists, Suzy appeared to be taking it all in her stride. Her floaty white summer dress made her look like a ballerina, and Lacey couldn't help but feel proud of all her young friend's achievements. How odd that she'd once thought of Suzy as a spoiled rich kid, because here she was, running a successful business in the most demanding of conditions.

Suzy embraced her. "I've not seen you in ages! How are you? Are you looking forward to your birthday? The big four-oh!"

"Don't remind me," Lacey replied. "I've been trying not to think about it. Besides, there's not much time to, with the festival."

"Gosh, I know," Suzy replied, glancing around. "We're rushed off our feet here, too. Fully booked all week and both weekends either side."

"That's amazing, Suzy," Lacey told her earnestly. "You deserve it for all your hard work."

Suzy grinned proudly. "So why are you here?" she asked. "I'm guessing you didn't come in for a quiet cuppa."

Lacey chuckled. "No. I was actually wondering if you might be able to help me with something."

"I can certainly try. What is it?"

"I'm holding an auction," Lacey explained. "Taryn seems to think there'll be more people interested in coming than I have the space for. Which got me thinking. I could put the auction online, and have people attend and bid virtually. Do you think you might be able to help me set that up?"

Suzy started to laugh. "What makes you think I can help?"

"Because you're young. All young people are good with technology."

"And since when did thirty-nine count as old?"

Lacey laughed. "When it comes to technology! Believe me. My technological competence is on a par with Gina's."

Suzy laughed again. "Well, funny you should mention that. My neighbor's kids are staying at the Lodge with me at the moment. Gabe, the younger one, just finished his A-Levels and was wasting his summer sitting in his room on his computer. The daughter decided to drop out of university. Basically, their parents got sick of it and asked me if I could give them some work here, you know, to see if a bit of hard graft might turn them into more rounded individuals." She chuckled wryly. "I needed help for the festival anyway, so I've put them up in the overnight staff rooms. Anyway, Gabe's a total tech genius. He's been headhunted to do a computer sciences degree at UCL. I bet he'll be able to help you. Oh, speak of the devil. Gabe!"

Lacey looked over. Coming down the staircase was a tall, lanky boy with long brown hair that hung around his ears and partly obscured his eyes. His oversized jeans hung too low on his backside, showing off more of his boxer shorts than Lacey cared to see.

He turned at the sound of his name being called, casting a wary eye over Suzy and Lacey.

"Gabe, come here a second!" Suzy insisted, with the sort of friendly enthusiasm teenage boys balked at.

He approached cautiously.

"Yeah?" he asked, head down, eyes on the floor.

"This is Lacey," Suzy said brightly. "She has an exciting work opportunity for you."

"I'm holding an auction," Lacey explained. "And I want to set up an online auction place where people can watch live and bid in real time, without having to be in the actual room." She struggled to put into words what she really wanted, looking at Gabe in the hopes he'd be able to fill in the blanks. "Does that make sense?"

"Yeah," was all he said.

"So it's not totally out of the realm of reality?" she pressed, attempting to get more clarification. "It's something a tech genius like you would be able to make?"

"Yeah," came his simple, monosyllabic reply.

Suzy jumped to Lacey's rescue. "I think what Lacey's trying to ask is whether she can hire you to do the work."

Gabe shrugged. "Sure."

Lacey looked over at Suzy, speechless with surprise. She couldn't quite believe this monosyllabic teen could make her pipe dream a reality, but it was a risk she was going to take.

She turned back to Gabe. "Wanna start now?"

Gabe flicked his fringe of greasy brown hair from his eyes and shrugged. "'K."

# CHAPTER ELEVEN

Lacey drove Gabe to her store, explaining the ins and outs of her vision as she went. Gabe barely said a word beyond grunting that he could definitely make the system as she wanted. Chester looked suspiciously from the back seat at the stranger sitting up front where he was supposed to.

As soon as Lacey entered the busy store, Gina put her hands on her hips and glared at her.

"What is going on?" she demanded. "Where have you been?"

Lacey gestured to Gabe. "Meet our newest staff member, Gabe. He's going to do some temporary computer work for us, setting up an online auction system."

Gina looked aghast at the lanky, greasy teenage boy standing next to Lacey. "And you made this decision without asking me?"

Gabe glanced awkwardly from one woman to the other, clearly uncomfortable to be caught in the middle of their conflict.

"I did," Lacey said.

"Because that's just what we need right now when we're so busy," Gina huffed. "More work."

Lacey frowned. Gina's reaction was worse than she'd been expecting. Yes, they were busy, but not too busy for one extra person. Gina had probably taken on more gardening work than she could manage, Lacey reasoned. She was spending more and more time out in the greenhouses, after all. She always got grumpy when she couldn't tend to her "special flower friends" as she called them.

"You're just going to have to trust me on this one, Gina," Lacey said with finality, ending the discussion there and then.

She led Gabe into the auction room.

"What do you think?" she said.

He grunted—the meaning indecipherable to Lacey—then sat, unfolded his laptop, perched it on his knees, and started tapping away at a million miles a second.

"Do you know how many people will be logging on?" he asked Lacey without looking away from the screen. "Because that will determine how much bandwidth I need."

"No, I don't," Lacey said, stammering over her words because she was so surprised to hear Gabe say so much in one go.

"Do you have a website? We can put out an ad and see how many hits it gets. That will give us a rough idea."

"Website? Yes, I have one of those. Somewhere ... "

Tom had helped her set it up. It was supposed to be idiot-proof, involving little more than choosing a pleasing color scheme, then dragging and dropping text boxes into place. It was still all a bit beyond Lacey, though.

She gave Gabe the address. He typed it in and her website popped onto his screen.

"Okay, no offense," Gabe muttered. "But your website sucks. So does your Wi-Fi connection. You need a better provider, just my two cents. How much traffic do you get on average?"

Lacey shrugged. "I don't know."

Gabe made a scoffing noise from the back of his throat. "Kinda vital information ... " he muttered under his breath.

Lacey bristled at his rudeness. But she reminded herself he was only a teenager. His frontal lobes weren't fully developed yet. And most geniuses had terrible social skills, didn't they? She'd have to give him a pass.

Gabe finally looked up at her. "Right. Here's my assessment. For this to work I need to sort out your internet first, then update the website, then find out how many people are interested, then go back to the internet and make sure there's enough bandwidth to host it, and then set up the system. Okay?"

Lacey blinked. She'd understood approximately ten percent of what Gabe was talking about. "Do whatever you have to do," she said, giving him free rein.

"'K,'" he grunted, turning his focus back to the screen.

He started tapping away again, falling completely silent, his whole attention absorbed by the task.

"Shall I come back later?" Lacey asked.

Gabe said nothing. She took that as answer enough, and headed back onto the main shop floor to patch things up with her disgruntled employee.

Gina stayed grumpy for the rest of the day, and Lacey was quietly relieved when the clock struck five and she could send her home. Once she was gone, Lacey headed back into the auction room to see how Gabe was getting on.

He glanced up briefly from his screen as she entered, then launched into a monologue without so much as a greeting.

"I set up a calendar to sync with yours, and it will tell you every time someone adds the event to their calendar."

Lacey hastened over and peered over his shoulder. He tapped away and showed her around a now seamless website, with a separate section about the upcoming auction and a visitor counter at the bottom of the page.

"Wait, you did all this in a day?" Lacey exclaimed. "It's like magic!"

Gabe didn't react to her comment. "I used the donkey from your poster so they know it's the same event."

"Oh," Lacey said, shaking her head. "No. Could you actually maybe change that? The donkey was a mistake."

She felt bad asking him to do more work, but Gabe shrugged like it was no big deal. "Sure. What do you want?"

"The Isidore Bonheur jockey sculpture would be better. It's the main piece on sale, and the biggest lure."

"This one?" Gabe asked. He'd already typed Isidore Bonheur into a search engine while she was speaking and pulled up a photograph of the sculpture.

"That's the one!" Lacey said, stunned by his speed.

He tippy-tapped again, and just like that, the image was displayed on her website. Lacey stopped herself from uttering "magic" again, since it hadn't gone down well the first time. But it really was magical to her.

"I'm adding some SEO," Gabe continued, his fingers flying over the keyboard like he was playing a piano. "That's search engine optimization. Basically it means when people search for bronze jockey sculpture, or jockey sculpture for sale, or auctions selling sculptures, et cetera, they're more likely to hit on it. See." He pointed at a string of numbers—one amongst several on his screen of computer code—that seemed to be multiplying.

"What am I looking at?" Lacey asked, clueless.

"IP addresses. Where people are located. They're all local so far, which probably means we've only reached people already here for the festival. I can do some other things to push your website up the search engine results, and open this thing out to the rest of the world."

"I'm fine with just Wilfordshire," Lacey quickly said, before he had the chance to start typing again and she was suddenly faced with an influx of global visitors. One thing at a time.

"'K," he said with his nonchalant shrug.

"What does that mean?" Lacey asked, pointing at the red exclamation point. "And the two hundred next to it?"

"That's an alert," Gabe explained. "It tells you how many people have synced the event to their personal calendar. We have one alert for people physically attending, another for virtual. That's the virtual one."

"You mean that's how many people will be watching me online?"

"Yup."

"But it says two hundred."

"Yup."

Lacey's mouth went suddenly dry. Taryn was right. There were way more people interested in the auction than she'd anticipated. Two hundred! She'd been expecting a few dozen more than her auction room could handle. But now it all felt extremely daunting. How would she manage a crowd that large? Especially the ones on the virtual platform?

"Anyway, that's everything done," Gabe mumbled, snapping his laptop shut. "The streaming stuff is self-explanatory really. You just turn everything on and press go."

He shrugged, like this was all so simple. But Lacey was in a tailspin.

"You have to come back," she stammered, feeling like she was suddenly lost at sea without a life raft, and this grunting teenager was her only chance of survival. "On auction day. Tomorrow. I'm useless with technology. What if it breaks down? I'll be so embarrassed."

Gabe gave a look of disdainful alarm. "I can come back," he said.

"You can?" Lacey asked, exhaling with relief. "Thank you. I'll pay you obviously. Thank you."

"Sure," he mumbled, scurrying away as if to get away from the crazy panicking woman.

The bell jangled as the door shut behind him, and Lacey looked over at Chester.

"Come on, boy," she said to her pooch, snatching up her keys. "I think we'd better get out of here before I go bananas."

They exited the store and Lacey locked everything up after her. To think, when she was back here tomorrow it would be auction day. Her third ever auction. Her third and most attended auction by a country mile!

The more she thought about it, the more she managed to whip herself into a frenzy over the number of people interested in the auction. She really needed a pep talk from Tom. Some reassurance. She was also still quietly carrying the burden of her new lead on her father on her shoulders, and it might be time to share it to let a bit of the pressure off.

She crossed the cobblestone street, Chester by her side, and weaved through the hordes of people toward the patisserie. If she'd thought the streets looked like a blown up liquor store before, now it looked as if a meteor made of wine and beer bottles had crashed into the middle of the street! Amber liquid ran between the cobblestones and into the gutters. And every which way she turned, there was another person, and another feathered fascinator to poke her in the eye. The festival really had turned Wilfordshire into a party town. It took her a good few minutes to negotiate her way through all the obstacles.

She pushed open the patisserie door, and the smell of baked goodies made her stomach growl. She suddenly realized just how hungry she was. She'd been too busy with her preparation to even stop for lunch today.

"Only me!" Lacey called as the bell tinkled above her.

Tom peeped his head out from around the kitchen partition. His eyes registered recognition and a huge grin lit up his face. "Lacey."

He still managed to look handsome, even after a long, grueling shift and while lightly dusted with flour.

Lacey maneuvered around the counter and entered the kitchen. The whole place was a mess of pots and pans. Discs of sponge cake in varying sizes—presumably the tiers of a wedding cake—sat cooling on the ledge. A big bowl of pink frosting sat beside them, the spoon still inside.

"How's it going?" she asked, eyeing the chaotic scenes.

Tom pointed at a pile of broken gingerbread horses, lying in halves like the front and back ends of pantomime costumes.

"Try one," he said. "That's the discard pile."

For obvious reasons, Lacey chose a front half. She popped it in her mouth. It tasted just like Tom's signature cookie dough but with the addition of spiced ginger, cinnamon, and cloves. And instead of just sugar, she picked up the distinctive flavor of dark molasses.

"Very good," she said through her mouthful, nodding her approval.

Tom grinned. "So are you all ready for your auction?"

"As ready as I'll ever be," Lacey said. "Suzy lent me a teenage tech genius to set up an online auction thing."

Tom carried on working as she spoke, taking a batch of doughy horses to the oven and replacing the silver tray of golden-colored ones with it. He laid the new, intact horses on the counter, and their gingery scent filled the room.

"That sounds very sci-fi," he said, his focus on his gingerbread cookies.

"It is. My auction room is full of cables and screens and devices."

Tom, peering intently at his gingerbread horses, didn't answer.

"So, anyway," Lacey continued, "I was just heading to Sakura's to pick up sushi for dinner. How about I get us one of those sashimi party boxes, and I can tell you all about it?"

Tom's eyes lit up. "That would be awesome. I haven't eaten since breakfast."

"You and me both."

Lacey headed out of the store, Chester trotting along beside her, and negotiated her way through the busy street to the Japanese takeaway. She and Tom often visited it on nights when they'd worked past closing time, because if there were any forty-piece sashimi sets left at the end of the day, they sold them for half price.

Lacey reached the cartoon pandas on the doors of Sakura's and pushed them open. But to her surprise, the shelves and fridges were completely empty.

A pretty Asian girl was wiping down the tables. She looked up at Lacey. "Sorry, we're all sold out this evening. The horsey people cleaned us out."

"No sashimi?" Lacey asked, surprised the festival crowd would visit a sushi bar decorated with cartoon panda bears. It didn't seem classy enough for them. And yet there wasn't a single sashimi party set in sight. There wasn't even an edamame pot or packet of wasabi peas!

The girl shook her head. "Sorry."

Lacey left, taking her cell phone out and dialing Tom. His phone kept ringing and ringing as she strolled the five minutes up the road. Eventually, she just let it go to voicemail.

"Bad news," she said. "There's no sushi so I'm going to the Cod Father."

Tom liked to pretend he was too much of a foodie for greasy chip shop food, but Lacey knew he secretly loved it.

But when Lacey reached the steamed up glass windows of the chippies she couldn't believe what she saw. It was full! Completely full. At least fifty young horsey people had taken over the place, their champagne bottles aloft, some dancing on the tables, others cheering like they were at a football match, still others engaged in a drunken food fight. Behind the counters, the Cod Father staff were watching on with tense smiles, clearly trying to weigh up the pros and cons of appeasing their unruly yet well-paying clientele.

Lacey grimaced. She wondered what the rich horsey parents would think of their offspring's antics. Even Chester had a look of distaste on his face as he watched them through the window.

Lacey tried to call Tom one more time. But once again, his phone just rang until his voicemail clicked on.

"Tom's phone. Please leave a message."

Lacey let out a sigh. "I've failed in my quest to find food," she told the recorder. "I'm giving up. Hope the cookies go well. I'll see you tomorrow."

She headed for home, hungry, and disappointed, only to discover all she had in the fridge was a Tupperware portion of tomato pasta. She reheated it as a stand-in dinner and called her sister, Naomi, for a pep talk.

"I'm holding an auction tomorrow. I'm really nervous."

"Well, I'm nervous about tomorrow, too," Naomi said. "I'm going on a date!"

How typical of her sister to turn the conversation to herself within two seconds.

"I have a good feeling about this one, Lacey," she continued. "He's absolutely dreamy. He works in property ... "

Lacey listened to her sister gush about what was likely to become another failed attempt to find The One, then went to bed with a knot of anxiety in her chest.

She stared at the ceiling, willing herself to sleep. But her nerves were stopping her from shutting down.

Then her phone binged and its bright blue light filled the room.

Sighing, Lacey rolled over in bed. The text was from Tom. She opened it.

*I just got your message. I'm so sorry! I got distracted and the next thing I knew it was the middle of the night. Good luck tomorrow with the auction. Love you.*

Lacey put her phone down without replying, and sunk back against the pillow with a huff. She wasn't really that mad at Tom, but she could do without the frustration of his busyness to add on top of the stress and nerves of hers.

She closed her eyes and tried some deep breathing exercises. But the sudden sound of bleating from outside put paid to that. Gina's sheep had obviously found their way into her garden.

Chester heard the noise as well and ran to the balcony window barking away. It wasn't his fault. He was hardwired to herd sheep, after all.

Lacey pressed a pillow over her head to try and drown out all the noises and disruptions, and after a few moments heard the sound of barking from outside that told her Gina had released Boudica to herd all the sheep back home.

When she did finally drift off to sleep, Lacey's brain rewarded her with a feverish dream in which she was chasing her father down the streets of Wilfordshire. No matter how fast she ran, he was always just out of reach. She could never quite catch him.

# Chapter Twelve

Lacey woke with a start. Her heart was pounding. Looking about her, she realized it was dawn. She checked the clock and saw it was not yet six a.m. But there was no point trying to sleep again. It was auction day. She may as well get a head start.

Chester whined at the disturbance of her getting out of bed too early.

"That's rich coming from you, mister," she said with a yawn, remembering his late night barking.

He followed her down to the kitchen and yawned sleepily as she put the coffee machine on.

As Lacey watched the glass jug fill up with coffee, her mind kept returning to the dream of her father.

She'd let the opportunity to learn more about him at Sawyer's slip through her fingers. She'd done the same with Xavier's Canterbury lead. With Xavier her reasoning had been his romantic interest in her. But she realized now she'd just been looking for an excuse. She'd felt no need to reject Colin, even though his interest in her was arguably more obvious.

She downed her espresso, then showered and dressed, all the while mulling over the cause of her hesitance. She was still ruminating as she led Chester down to the beach.

"It's fear, isn't it?" she said to the ocean.

Fear she'd hit yet another dead end? Or fear she wouldn't? That this time, she would find him, and with it, the truth of his abandonment?

"I should call Xavier," she said, realizing she would drive herself crazy if she didn't take some kind of action. It was seven thirty in Spain, so he'd probably be awake. But what could she say? "Sorry for ghosting you all summer, but now I need your help?" No. It was far too awkward. She opted, instead, for a text message.

*I found a new lead on my father. An antique contact thinks he may have opened a store in Canterbury.*

A minute later, her phone buzzed with a reply.

*I will look into it.*

She tried not to overanalyze the simplicity of his message. The important thing was he was still willing to help.

Despite the early hour, the sun was bright and strong. Lacey reached the store and opened it up for the day, deciding to prop the front door open in order to let the air circulate.

"You'll have to be the bell today," she said to Chester as she repositioned a heavy statue to use as a doorstop.

Immediately, he took up position by the door, looking very self-important.

Lacey wasn't expecting any customers for at least an hour, so was shocked when a smartly dressed woman appeared in the doorway.

She looked to be in her late fifties or early sixties, but the discrepancy between the lines on her face and her neck indicated she'd had a face lift or two in her time. She had the distinctive cheeks of someone who'd had fat injected into them, and the sort of perfectly straight nose someone could only get from the skilled hands of a surgeon in South Korea's Gangnam Province. Her pouty lips suggested regular fillers, and were accentuated further by water-effect lip gloss. She had the same aura as Taryn—confident, busy, and only partly present.

"Can I help you?" Lacey asked, looking up at her.

"I heard about your auction," the woman said, pointing at the poster. Her voice was brusque, and she had a Russian-sounding accent. "I want to reserve a seat. Front row."

Lacey straightened up. No one had ever asked to reserve a seat at one of her auctions before! It was quite exciting. Or at least, it would be if the woman asking wasn't quite so intimidating.

"Of course," Lacey said, leading her inside and over to the counter where she grabbed her pen and a notebook. "Can I take your name?"

"It's Ms. Oxana Kovalenko," the woman said. "That's Oxana with an X."

Lacey made a note. "I'll put this on a seat to reserve it," she said.

"Good. How much do I owe you?"

Lacey frowned. "Owe me? What for?"

"The reservation," Oxana said, flapping a hand as if to hurry her along. She was giving off the air of having other important things to attend to.

"There's no charge," Lacey said, shaking her head.

Oxana looked surprised. Clearly wherever she was from, this was not usual practice.

"In that case, can I pick the seat?" Oxana said.

Lacey couldn't think of any reason to refuse. "Sure," she said.

Oxana looked pleased, as if she thought Lacey was giving her special treatment because of how important she was.

Lacey led her into the auction room. The woman walked around glancing about her like she was attending an estate sale rather than an auction.

"You'll keep the windows open, won't you?" Oxana said. "It'll get too hot otherwise. What are the screens for?"

"The auction is being broadcast online," Lacey said. "There'll be some virtual attendees."

"Huh," Oxana said, in a voice that could either be impressed or disdainful, since she was so hard to read. She waltzed toward the front of the hall, her heels clacking loudly. She pointed at a seat. "I want THAT one."

Lacey went over and placed the handwritten sign on the seat. "It's all yours."

Oxana nodded with satisfaction.

In just the few short minutes Lacey had spent in Oxana Kovalenko's company, she'd gotten quite a good understanding of the type of woman she was. A Saskia. Someone who was used to getting her own way. A businesswoman. But she was curious about who exactly she was, and her curiosity, as it often did, got the better of her.

"May I ask what you do for a living?" she asked.

A look of pride appeared on Oxana's face. "I'm surprised you don't recognize me. I won Ukraine's wealthiest female CEO of an Industrial, Plastics or Textile company award three years running."

Unsurprisingly, Lacey didn't recognize her. It wasn't like she made a habit of reading the Ukrainian version of the Forbes Rich List.

"How fascinating," she said. "Well, I look forward to seeing you later for the auction."

Oxana gave her a peculiar look, as if no one in her life had ever said they were looking forward to seeing her again. She almost smiled. Almost, but not quite.

"Yes. Okay," was all she said, before she turned on her heel and marched away.

If Oxana was in any way representative of what was to come, Lacey got the distinct impression she was going to meet some very colorful and interesting characters today.

There was still a bit of time before Gabe arrived, so Lacey checked through her agenda, rehearsed her opening lines, and warmed up her voice—auctioneering could be very taxing on the vocal cords.

She was in the middle of lip trilling when she was interrupted by the sound of Chester barking.

She headed onto the shop floor to discover that Chester had left his post by the door and was now running circles around a dog. It was an English shepherd, just like him.

Bemused, Lacey looked around. She couldn't see its accompanying human anywhere.

"Where did you come from?" she asked the dog.

By the way it was allowing Chester to run circles around it, Lacey guessed it was older and more mature than he was.

The penny suddenly dropped just at the same time a very familiar male voice called from the street outside, "Stella? Stella, where did you go?"

Through the open door, Lacey saw him pacing around the cobblestone streets looking lost. She couldn't quite believe it.

Colin was here.

Lacey was stunned. Why was Colin in Wilfordshire? Had he come all this way just to see her?

"Stella?" he called. "Stella, where are you?"

At the sound of her master's voice, Stella began to bark. Colin turned and looked straight through the open door at Lacey.

Their gazes locked. A wide smile spread across his lips.

Lacey felt a lump of anticipation form in her throat as he walked in through the doorway.

"So this is your store," he said, confidently strolling in.

"Colin?" Lacey said. "What are you doing here?"

"I heard about this little auction," he replied, as he ruffled Stella's ears in his hands. "Equestrian themed. There's an Isidore Bonheur sculpture in bronze that I'd very much like to add to my collection."

A whole mix of emotions churned inside of Lacey; suspicion that Colin was using the statue as an excuse to see her again; excitement that someone might find her so desirous they'd drive several hours for a chance to see her again; then guilt for even entertaining such a thought.

"You came to bid on the statue?" she asked.

"That's right. But I think I'm in the wrong place, as there appears to be a donkey on the poster..."

Lacey couldn't help but laugh. "You're in the right place," she said. "But just at the wrong time. We don't kick off for another two hours." She handed him one of the printed item lists. "Here are all the lots for the day."

"Thanks," Colin said. "I'll take a look down at the beach. Seems like nice weather for a beach day. What do you think, Stella? Shall we go to the beach?"

As he spoke to his dog, Lacey remembered what he'd told her about Stella being too elderly to attend auctions anymore, and wondered why he'd really brought her along. Perhaps because he knew their dogs would be drawn to one another? As a lure?

Her musings were interrupted by the arrival of Gabe. He was early. He marched in carrying his big black case of equipment, his jeans slung low. Without so much as a hello, he gave Colin and Lacey a suspicious look as he advanced.

Colin stepped back toward the door. "I'll catch you later," he said, before leaving with Stella.

Gabe crossed the store and into the auction room. Lacey followed him.

"Is that your boyfriend?" Gabe asked as he put his case down and began unpacking a bunch of thick black cables.

"He's just a friend," Lacey replied.

"Sure," Gabe said. "That was a platonic look if ever I saw one ... "

He was being sarcastic and Lacey didn't like his insinuation one bit.

"I'm in a relationship," she refuted, hands on hips.

Gabe looked over at her from the camcorder he was setting up. "Maybe someone should tell him that."

# CHAPTER THIRTEEN

"The name's Dustin Powell," the bald man at the counter said.

Lacey typed his name into her database while Gina handed him his corresponding bidder's card.

"Congratulations, Mr. Powell," Lacey said cordially. "You're bidder number one for the day."

"Lucky number one, I hope," he said with a chuckle.

Lacey handed him the item list. "This is everything we'll be auctioning today," she explained, feeling a mix of anticipation, nerves, and excitement that the wheels were now in motion.

One day, Lacey would like to use the same system as Sawyer & Sons and have all the lots on actual display for attendees to peruse at their leisure. But with a grand total of two staff members, it currently wasn't possible. Yet. Considering how quickly she'd managed to get an online system set up, maybe it was more possible than Lacey realized.

More people started entering through the main door. They were all dressed to the nines, as if her auction was another official festival event on the calendar. There were feathered fascinators galore!

Gina flashed Lacey an excited look as a queue started to form. Soon, all eyes would be on her. And what a lot of eyes ...

She swallowed the nervous lump forming in her throat.

"Are you okay to carry on with the registration process?" she asked Gina. "I need to start letting people into the auction room."

"Of course," Gina said with a nod.

Lacey left the counter. Dustin Powell and attendees number two and three followed after her into the auction room.

As they chose their seats, Lacey went over to the pulpit. She'd set herself up by the French doors, reasoning that the summer sun streaming through would make the merchandise look even more alluring. But now she was relieved for the fresh air; attendees four, five, and six were choosing their seats, and they'd brought a whole load of competing expensive perfume and cologne smells wafting in with them.

Gabe had set himself up on the other side of the French doors. He was surrounded by a messy spider web of black cables and electronic gadgets. It was hard to see where man ended and machine began. Indeed, he seemed so interconnected with the whole thing it was as if he was some kind of bionic man.

Lacey would've preferred to have squirreled him away in the back office out of sight, but since he was monitoring all the equipment needed for the live feed, as well as the online system throughout the auction, it made sense for him to be close by. He'd given Lacey a tablet she could keep on the pulpit with her in case she wanted a closer look at the virtual attendees, but since that clearly wasn't enough for the young technophile, he'd also set up a projector screen to beam the attendees onto. There was already a patchwork quilt of faces on it, at least as many people on the screen as there now were in the room.

Among the crowd, Lacey noticed Mr. Oolong from the Lodge, and Monsieur Cheval of the tantrumming wife fame. She grew even more nervous as she recalled their unpleasant personalities. Hopefully they were in slightly more reasonable moods today than they had been when she'd first met them.

She paced along the aisle she'd left between the chairs, which was reminiscent of a wedding, and peeked around the wall to the main floor. There were now around thirty to forty people in the queue waiting to get their bidder's cards. Lacey's heart started slamming in her chest.

Gina spotted her. "Are you okay, dear?" she asked, somehow managing to talk and type at the same time. It was the sort of multitasking abilities that made Gina an expert gardener. "You look stressed."

"I am," Lacey said in a hushed voice. "There are so many people."

"That's a good thing," Gina whispered back. "Just think how financially lucrative this auction is going to be. And channel all that nervous energy into your performance."

Lacey nodded. It was the same advice Naomi was always giving her.

"You've got this," Gina added.

Grateful for the pep talk, Lacey took a breath and headed back into the auction room.

She took her place at the pulpit, watching the room fill with men, women, and feathered fascinators. She spotted Colin (with Stella) enter and flashed him a friendly wave. He waved back and took an aisle seat.

Soon, every seat bar one was filled. Right at the front was the empty reserved seat of Oxana Kovalenko.

Just then, a hush fell over the audience. The whole energy of the room seemed to change in an instant. The sound of heels clacking slowly on the floorboards made everyone turn toward the door. And there was Oxana.

She waltzed in like she owned the place, like she was the bride walking the aisle in a tight navy dress and nude Louboutins. She made no hurry to take her seat, acting like the VIP at a fashion show. The reserved front row seat only added to the illusion.

The woman lowered herself into the chair directly in front of Lacey, and she regretted having given Oxana free rein to pick her seat. Her unreadable hawk-like eyes burned into Lacey. But what was done was done, and Lacey wasn't about to let one formidable business tycoon put her off her game.

She grabbed her gavel, filled with determination. It was now or never!

"Welcome, everyone," she announced, projecting her voice through the room. "It's great to have you all here. Or virtually here," she added, addressing the camera feed.

The attendees gave an appreciative titter of laughter. Bolstered, Lacey continued.

"I know you're all excited to see the Isidore Bonheur, but as you can see from your item lists, we have some really fantastic items to show you first. There are some real gems here, and a lot to get through, so let's get cracking. We'll begin with this beautiful dark tan, Swaine-Brigg antique riding bag, complete with its original silver canteen."

She revealed the first bag to the audience, assessing their expressions to see how interested they were. They were fairly unreadable, like poker players. Not the usual auction crowd, that was for sure. Still, she'd paid about thirty for each of the bags, but knew in the right conditions they could fetch close to one hundred, so decided to start at a safe-ish fifty.

"Let's start the bidding at fifty," she announced.

To her surprise, more hands than she could count went into the air. On the projector screen, several of the patchwork squares started flashing, demanding her attention.

"Oh!" Lacey exclaimed. "It's going to be one of those days, is it?"

The audience laughed appreciatively.

Lacey pointed at bidder twenty-two, accepting them as the fifty-pound bid, then suggested, "Fifty-five?"

Not a single person dropped out the race. She'd need to make the increments bigger.

"Fifty-five to bidder fourteen," she announced. "Can I get sixty-five pounds?"

A few bidding cards dropped, but there were still a good few dozen in the room, and at least ten more virtual attendees wanting to bid.

Sixty-five became eighty, ninety, and then one hundred. Lacey couldn't believe it. This was only the first item!

"Can I get one hundred and five?" Lacey said, glancing about at the still room. "One hundred and four? Three? Two? One?" She chuckled, as no one else put in a bid. "Sold!" she announced, banging the gavel. "One hundred pounds to bidder number sixteen."

The final bidder was a big woman with short gray hair and dangling gem-stoned earrings. She nodded in acknowledgment of her win, and Lacey noted down her bidder number, ecstatic to see the first item had sold for so much more than she'd paid the leather store man for it.

"Next, we have these nineteenth-century Latin American spurs," she announced. "Sturdy iron with working rowels. Let's start the bidding at one hundred forty pounds."

She'd bought them for seventy, but since the Swaine-Brigg had gone so high, she decided to start the bidding way higher than she usually would.

There was just as much interest in the antique spurs as there had been in the saddle bag, which Lacey found even more surprising considering there was much less practical use for them. Maybe Gina was right when she'd said these types of people just really liked spending money.

Lacey accepted the first bid and took a calculated risk, announcing, "Can I get one sixty?"

She was expecting some kind of reaction from the audience that she'd increased the price by such a large increment, but they barely even blinked. It started to dawn on Lacey that one hundred and sixty pounds was chump change to these people. Heck, six hundred pounds probably was, too!

She accepted the one sixty pound bid, and moved up to one eighty. Mr. Oolong secured the one eighty bid, so she pushed it up to two hundred, which was also accepted by Monsieur Cheval.

"Two fifty," Lacey suggested, making an ever bigger leap.

Mr. Oolong accepted the price without even blinking. In fact, if she was reading his expression right, it seemed that the higher the price went, the more he enjoyed it...

Lacey suddenly realized what was going on. They were showing off! Competing! This wasn't the usual auction clientele after a bargain. The horsey people were specifically here to show off just how wealthy they were to one another!

"Three hundred," Lacey announced.

Bidder twenty-three—a pompous-looking older man sporting a painfully red sunburn—flashed his card.

"Three hundred," Lacey acknowledged. She looked back to Mr. Oolong, the other bidder still in the two horse race. "Four hundred?"

He shook his head. Ah! So there was a bottom to his pockets after all.

"Three fifty?" Lacey amended.

He nodded and flashed his card.

Lacey turned to the sunburnt elderly man. "Three eighty?" she asked.

He shook his head.

"Three seventy?"

Another shake.

"Three sixty?"

He started to chuckle and shook his head again, indicating he was giving up entirely.

Lacey smiled and turned to Mr. Oolong. "Sold for three hundred and fifty pounds!" she announced, banging the gavel.

As she noted his number next to the item she couldn't quite believe she'd made such a good profit on the spurs, all thanks to a grouchy man with a taste for obscure tea.

Lacey started feeling giddy from the high of it. She'd turned such a large profit on the first few items, she couldn't even fathom how the rest of the auction would progress. Maybe all the horsey people would get bored of showing off to each other? Or maybe they'd just get even more competitive as time went on. There was only one way to find out!

The rest of the antique riding equipment sold just as well—the entire ten-piece WWI cavalry riding boots sold to Dustin Powell, aka lucky bidder number one. All the while, Lacey kept one eye on Oxana in the front row, who seemed to be bidding without rhyme or reason, never securing a win.

"Let's move on to my personal favorite items on sale today," Lacey said. "The art."

She noticed Colin smile as she announced the first David Alfaro Siqueiros painting, the item she'd beaten him to at the Sawyer & Sons auction. She'd bought the pair for seven hundred in total, and wondered how much she might fetch for them here. The horsey folk certainly appreciated antique objets d'art, but they might not be so keen on the paintings she'd selected. It was an eclectic mix, after all, from the oil landscapes of John Mace, the Mabel Gear watercolors, and the Alexandre Pau De Saint Martin graphite master sketch.

"This gorgeous piece was created with shoe polish," Lacey told the audience. "And I'd like to start the bidding at four hundred."

A sea of hands rose into the air. On the projector a whole bunch of the little screens flashed. So there was going to be a fierce bidding war for the art as well, it seemed.

Amongst the people in the audience, Lacey noted that Colin had put in a bid. She pointed to him first, smiling to acknowledge the auction they'd attended together. Then Lacey took a breath and launched into it.

"We have four hundred, can I get four fifty. Four fifty there to bidder twelve. Five hundred? Yes, five hundred accepted to virtual bidder sixteen. Five fifty? Five fifty to you, sir. Six hundred?"

On and on it went, the price racing up as if money was no object to the attendees. She noted that Colin dropped out pretty quickly, followed by the rest of the bidders in the room. The bidding went to the virtual attendees, before finally settling at seven hundred and twenty pounds. It was an enormous windfall for Lacey.

Then she felt an excited rumble in her stomach. It was time for the Isidore Bonheur. Unlike the majority of the other items, the bronze sculpture was displayed in all its glory on a plinth. It looked alluring in the summer sun.

"And here it is," she announced. "The Isidore Bonheur! Isidore Bonheur was one of the nineteenth century's most distinguished French animalier sculptors and this gorgeous bronze jockey statue on marble base is one of his most commercially successful pieces. Standing at twenty-three inches tall and twenty-two inches wide, this one is in excellent condition, with no scratches or wear." She thought back to the wonderful moment she'd found the sculpture in the small little art store on the cherry tree–lined street, and was overcome with romantic nostalgia. "Let's start the bidding at three thousand," she announced.

No sooner were the words out of Lacey's mouth than she regretted them. She'd gotten lost in the moment and started too high. She was expecting to hear an audible gasp, or worse, laughter. But to her surprise, her starting bid was met by a sea of paddles. It seemed as if everyone wanted the sculpture—every person in the room and every one online, too!

"In that case, let's start the bidding at three thousand five hundred," Lacey amended, not quite believing what she was saying.

A couple of hands dropped, but, to Lacey's astonishment, there were still too many for her to begin the bidding in earnest. She only had two eyes and one brain; she needed to wean down the masses to at least a manageable amount before she began!

"Four thousand five hundred," she announced, hearing the pitch begin to rise in her voice.

Finally, with the starting bid at over double the price Lacey had originally paid for the sculpture, around half the hands in the room had lowered, and most of the patchwork screens were no longer flashing.

There were five interested parties left. Four in the room—Oxana, Dustin Powell, Monsieur Cheval, and Colin (gazing at her with his distractingly mysterious smile), and one on the screen, someone who'd chosen not to show his face, but just his username—Hugh Buckingham. He definitely sounded like a rich horsey person with a name like that, and Lacey wondered why he was staying anonymous. Perhaps he was hideously disfigured, she mused, getting giddy and carried away in the moment. Or maybe he was just sitting in the Coach House Inn pub, enjoying a nice pint of ale while he placed his bids. She made a mental note to ask Gabe to check his IP address after the auction, just to satisfy her curiosity.

Lacey pointed her gavel first to Colin. It only seemed fair, since he'd missed out on buying the sculpture in Weymouth because of her, though if he wanted it *that* much, Lacey didn't understand why he didn't just make a counteroffer at the time, rather than waiting for her to auction it and drive the price up so high.

He nodded in acceptance of the price, and a small smile played across his lips. Lacey quickly looked away, feeling a blush rising in her cheeks.

Her eyes fell straight to Oxana.

"Four thousand six hundred?" she asked.

The woman nodded.

Of all the people at the auction, Lacey was loath to sell the amazing sculpture to Oxana. The mean woman surely wouldn't appreciate it. She probably had a thousand and one other artworks in her Ukrainian mansion, and the Isidore Bonheur would just sit there gathering dust. She desperately wanted it to go to someone who'd cherish it.

She looked at the jolly face of Dustin Powell. "Four thousand seven hundred?" she asked.

He nodded.

Lacey swallowed the lump in her throat. This was going far beyond her wildest expectations.

She looked at Monsieur Cheval next. He was sweating and tugging at his shirt collar. "Four thousand eight hundred?"

To her shock, he stood, threw his bidder's paddle onto his chair, and stormed away.

Keeping her cool, Lacey simply moved on to Hugh Buckingham and repeated the offer. "Four thousand eight hundred?"

His screen flashed as he accepted the bid.

She worked around the room. With just four people left in the bidding, Lacey slowed the increments, but the fight remained fierce. Dustin dropped out at four thousand nine hundred, leaving the final three to push the price to the brink of five thousand.

Lacey's mind was so giddy she could hardly even keep up with it. It felt like she was in some kind of dream!

"Four thousand nine hundred and fifty?" she asked Colin, hearing her voice saying the words but not fully comprehending she'd reached such dizzying heights.

The man slowly shook his head. He looked crestfallen. Lacey couldn't help but feel bad for him. He'd lost out on the statue again. She wondered, once more, why he hadn't even tried to out heckle her back at the Weymouth art store. She'd never have shelled out five thousand pounds for the statue. Two had felt like too much of a risk. He could easily have outpriced her if he was willing to go up so high for it.

Lacey also felt bad for herself. She'd have preferred to sell the statue to Colin, who clearly had a passion for it since he'd followed it across counties. Instead, she was left with two bidders: Oxana, looking pinched and stern in the first row, and the faceless Hugh Buckingham.

Since he'd chosen not to connect via his web camera, his name flashed every time he put in his bid, and his screen was flashing now to indicate he wanted to take Colin's unclaimed bid.

"Four thousand nine hundred and fifty pounds," Lacey accepted. She looked to Oxana. "Four thousand nine hundred and sixty pounds?"

Oxana nodded, but she appeared to be growing visibly frustrated.

"Four thousand nine hundred and seventy?" Lacey asked the faceless Hugh Buckingham.

Oxana glowered over her shoulder at the projector. Hugh's screen flashed in acceptance. Oxana threw her arms in the air.

"Four thousand nine hundred and seventy?" she asked.

Oxana nodded.

Back to Hugh. "Four thousand nine hundred and eighty?" Lacey asked. His screen flashed.

Back to Oxana. "Four thousand nine hundred and ninety?"

Oxana gritted her teeth. Her pupils were dilated, giving her an eagle-like expression. She was clearly moments away from throwing in the towel.

But she nodded, and Lacey took the bid.

She turned to the screen. "Can I get five thousand?" she asked, hearing her voice come out high-pitched in disbelief it had really gotten this far.

The screen flashed.

A hubbub rippled around the whole room. The audience seemed to be enjoying this tense tennis match, and Lacey was glad for the excitement, because it helped temper her own giddiness that she was about to make such a huge windfall on the gorgeous statue.

She looked at Oxana and opened her mouth, about to announce the next increment.

But Oxana beat her to it.

"Five thousand and one pounds," she announced loudly, her strong accent seeming to reach the far corners of the room.

The hubbub turned to whispers of astonishment. Lacey couldn't stop herself from raising an eyebrow. Never before had someone so brazenly interrupted her like that with a counter-bid. And such a petty one as well!

Still, Lacey didn't have much choice but to accept the bid.

"Five thousand and one pounds," she said.

A nasty smile spread across Oxana's lips.

# CHAPTER FOURTEEN

As unsatisfying as a pound by pound bidding war was for Lacey, it was still profit and not to be scoffed at. Besides, it seemed to entertain the crowd, who loved a good back and forth like it was a tennis match.

With Oxana's one-pound higher bid, Lacey turned her attention back to her virtual attendee, Hugh Buckingham.

"Five thousand and two pounds?" she offered, adding the petty one-pound increment Oxana's bid had forced her hand to make.

Nothing happened. Lacey tried again. Perhaps he'd not heard. "Can I get five thousand and two pounds?"

Still, no bid came.

Lacey frowned. So far, Hugh had been very quick on the draw. Lacey couldn't believe that he'd drop out over a single pound. Even if he had a budget, one pound surely hadn't pushed him over it.

A second passed. Then two. Then three.

In the front, Oxana raised a single eyebrow at Lacey, looking extremely unimpressed by her hesitation. And fair enough, really, Lacey had to admit. It wasn't like she'd hesitated at any other point before now.

Quickly, Lacey glanced over at Gabe to see if there was any sign of him having issues with the virtual auction platform. He caught her eye and shrugged. Presumably that meant everything was in working order as far as he was concerned.

A good ten seconds had passed now. Lacey had no choice. She couldn't delay the sale just because she didn't like the bidder. The gorgeous Isidore Bonheur statue was going to the Ukrainian businesswoman whether she wanted it to or not.

She looked at the smirking Oxana and brought down the gavel. "Sold for five thousand ... and *one* pounds."

The audience erupted into applause and Lacey took comfort that at least they'd enjoyed it, even if she was internally grimacing. Oxana also looked extremely self-satisfied.

"That's everything," Lacey announced. "Thank you so much for attending. It will take us a little bit of time to organize all your items and handle the packing and paperwork, so please feel free to head out for lunch and return at a convenient time later."

The auction attendees stood and began filing out, thanking Lacey as they left and chatting amongst themselves about the items they'd acquired. Some seemed thrilled with their purchases, others bitter to have missed out.

Lacey lost sight of Colin in the din.

Gina headed to the main shop floor to attend to the few attendees who'd stayed behind, and Lacey went into her office to prepare their receipts.

She was buzzing from the auction. It had been such a high.

She scanned through the logs and quickly calculated that she'd taken in significantly more than she'd anticipated. But she was still confused about Hugh Buckingham dropping out of the bidding and letting Oxana win by a single pound.

Just then, there came a knock at her office door. Lacey looked over to see Colin.

"There you are," she said. "I wondered where you'd disappeared to. I'm sorry you missed out on the sculpture again."

Colin walked into the room. "That's okay. I won something better."

"You did?" Lacey asked. She couldn't recall Colin having won any of his bids, but then again, she'd been in such a heady daze maybe she'd just forgotten. She looked back down to her notes trying to see what he was referring to. "What did you win?"

"An opportunity," Colin said.

Lacey looked at him, frowning with confusion. "I don't understand. An opportunity to ... "

But before she finished speaking, Colin leaned forward, lips puckered, and attempted to kiss her.

Lacey was stunned. She immediately put her hands up to stop him. "Colin, no. I'm sorry but I think you've misunderstood."

She shook her head and he backed off.

Colin looked extremely embarrassed. Lacey felt her cheeks burning, too.

"Goodness," he said, scratching his neck. "I'm sorry. I guess I misread the signs."

But before either had a chance to say any more, a sudden commotion sounded from the shop floor. Angry voices. Barking dogs.

Lacey exchanged a confused look with Colin.

"Excuse me," she said, hurrying past him to see what on earth was going on.

She reached the shop floor to discover the most peculiar sight. A man in pajamas and a bathrobe was shouting at Gina, and both dogs were barking frantically at him.

Lacey quickly deduced that the man hadn't been at the auction—there was no way she would have failed to notice a man in slippers and a bathrobe! Nor would she forget one who was so clearly unwell. The man's face was flushed with fever. Sweat beaded his forehead.

But who on earth was he? Some random madman who'd wandered in off the streets to shout gibberish?

The handful of auction attendees who'd stayed to pay and collect their items watched on with astonishment as poor Gina bore the brunt of the angry man's diatribe.

"Excuse me," Lacey demanded, marching toward him. "What is going on?"

"There you are," the man said, pointing an angry finger at her. "You are a cheating fraudster."

As the man's finger now pointed angrily at Lacey, Chester started barking even more sternly. He wanted to protect his owner.

"It's okay, Chester," she told him.

The dog started to calm down, which had a knock-on effect of calming Boudica too. At the same time, Colin emerged from the back room and tamed his own growling pooch.

With the sound of barking ceased, Lacey could finally think clearly.

"Do I know you?" she asked, affronted by his accusation.

"I'm Hugh Buckingham," he said. "And you, dear girl, are a cheat!"

Lacey put it all together. This was Hugh Buckingham, the virtual attendee who'd missed out on the Isidore Bonheur by a pound. Clearly, he hadn't attended the auction in person because he was sick. But why was he calling her a cheat? A fraud?

"I don't understand what you're accusing me of," she said. "What have I cheated you out of?"

"Take a look for yourself!" Hugh shouted, waving a piece of paper at her. "I have the proof!"

Lacey snatched it from him angrily, ready to see whatever proof he apparently had of her so-called cheating.

She squinted, confused about what she was looking at. It was an image of her auction, a computer screenshot with a time stamp in the corner. It showed her holding the gavel, about to bring it down to award the Isidore Bonheur statue to Oxana. But the screenshot also showed Hugh's interface, and very clearly showed he had put in a bid.

"That can't be right," she said, frowning. She was certain his screen hadn't lit up again after Oxana's petty one-pound increase. She'd even been looking for it, hoping for it, so she wouldn't have to sell the statue to the frustrating businesswoman.

"Are you calling me a liar?" Hugh accused.

His illness was making him look quite deranged, with bloodshot eyes and a strange waxy quality to his pale skin. Lacey would very much like to get him out of her store before he infected her and everyone else within spitting distance with his sickness.

"Not at all," she said, still confused. "I don't know what's going on here." She beckoned Gabe over and showed him the screenshot. "Any idea what happened here?"

Gabe shrugged dismissively. "You can do anything with Photoshop these days. He probably screen printed the image then changed the timestamp."

Lacey winced. She should've anticipated the teenager with terrible social skills would say the wrong thing. And not just the wrong thing, absolutely the worst thing he could have!

Hugh's pale face turned so red he looked like he was about to pop.

"I did not doctor the image!" he bellowed. "I put my bid in after the pound increase and it was completely ignored!"

Lacey tried to temper the man's frustration. "Is there any chance there was a glitch?" she asked Gabe.

Now it was Gabe's turn to look furious. "Are you suggesting my coding was wrong?"

"Not at all," Lacey said, feeling very much like she was stuck between a rock and a hard place. "I'm just spitballing here. Because something's happened somewhere, and we need to get to the bottom of it."

Gabe glowered. "I'll look into it," he said, retreating grumpily to the auction room.

Lacey turned back to Hugh. He coughed into the crook of his elbow.

"How long will this take?" he demanded through his splutters. "I need to get back to bed."

"Then you probably should," Lacey told him. "There's not a lot we can do right now."

But Hugh shook his head petulantly. "No way. I don't trust you or that greasy-haired oik to find the truth. I'm not leaving here without my statue."

Lacey ground her teeth. She was furious with the situation. Gabe had assured her this would be foolproof. But here she was in a very awkward and messy situation, very much looking like a fool.

Hugh continued his rant. "I won't take no for an answer. I refuse to. The statue is mine. That woman was quite clearly backing down. Increasing the bid by one pound? She was obviously losing her cool! I can give you the extra two pounds right now."

Lacey shook her head. "I'm sorry, but it's too late. I can't back out now. It's against the rules."

At that moment, Lacey noticed Oxana standing in the doorway of the store. By the expression on her face, she'd been standing there the whole time watching Hugh's outburst.

Oxana walked across the length of the store, and Hugh looked at her like he wasn't sure whether she was really there or if she'd been conjured by his feverish mind.

She calmly reached the counter. "I'm here to collect my statue," she said to Lacey.

Great. If there was any way for this situation to get any more tense, this was it!

"Maybe you should come back a little later," Gina said.

"Absolutely not," Oxana replied. "I think you'll find I sent an immediate payment for the statue, and it's my legal right to take it with me."

Lacey checked her bank account. Oxana was telling the truth. Lacey had never felt so frustrated to have such a large sum deposited into her business account! But with the uncertainty as to the true owner of the statue, it only added an extra layer of confusion. Because now there was no way she could stop Oxana from walking out of the store with the statue, and appealing to her on a personable level was quite clearly useless. Oxana had nothing to lose by taking the statue with her, and everything to lose by being "polite" and leaving it in Lacey's possession until such a time as the dispute could be resolved.

Oxana looked at Lacey expectantly. "Well? Can I have my statue?"

Gina looked at Lacey questioningly, her eyes silently asking what to do.

Completing the triad of expectant glances was Hugh. Only he was staring at Lacey furiously. "You're not letting her leave with it? I'll never see it again!"

"I don't have a choice," Lacey said.

She retrieved the wrapped parcel from behind the counter.

With a nasty smile, Oxana snatched it up in her arms.

"Tough luck, buttercup," she said to Hugh, then began marching toward the door. As she went, she exclaimed, "I'm going to the pub to celebrate my win!" before pausing at the threshold, turning on her heel, and blowing Hugh a kiss. Then she was gone.

Lacey could not believe what she'd just witnessed. The pettiness of the woman, to win by a single pound and then taunt Hugh to his face over it!

"I'm so sorry about that," Lacey began.

Her apology was cut short, because Hugh Buckingham turned on Lacey and unleashed his fury.

"I'll ruin you," he said, pointing his finger right in her face. "Just you wait and see. I'll end you and this stupid excuse for an auction house! You made a bad decision when you made Hugh Buckingham your enemy!"

Lacey's heart thumped. But suddenly Colin was there. He must've been watching from the sidelines, and had only now decided to step in and play the Knight in Shining Armor.

"That's enough," he announced, turning Hugh around and marching him out into the street.

But even that didn't stop Hugh. He just continued his rant from there, with hundreds of festival attendees witnessing it all.

"This establishment cannot be trusted!" he screamed. "It is run by a thief and a liar! I urge you not to shop here!"

Colin manhandled Hugh through the crowds, his angry screams audible long after he was out of sight.

# CHAPTER FIFTEEN

"Here," Gina said, placing a mug of tea on the counter in front of Lacey. "Honey and lemon."

Lacey flashed her friend a grateful smile.

On Gina's insistence, Lacey had locked up the store following Hugh's outburst. It was only once she was alone that she realized just how shaken she was. The altercation had come so quickly off the back of Colin's unwanted kiss attempt, which itself had come right off the back of her auction high, Lacey was feeling scrambled and unsettled.

She took a sip of tea. It was far more bitter than she was expecting.

"Honey and lemon?" she questioned Gina.

"And a wee dram of whiskey," her friend replied with a wink. She took the stool next to Lacey. "How are you doing?" she asked her, kindly.

"My nerves are shot."

"I'm not surprised. It's not like following the rules did you any favors. You would have made more money selling it to Hugh, and Oxana wasn't the most gracious of winners either."

Lacey heard a knock on the window. She looked up, about to call out, "We're closed," when she realized it was Taryn standing there.

"What does she want?" Lacey muttered.

Gina looked up. "I'll get rid of her," she said.

She went over to the door, unlocking it, but Taryn shoved right past her. She earned herself a growl from both Chester and Boudica.

"Lacey, are you okay?" Taryn exclaimed in her fake friendly way. "I heard all the dogs barking and a man yelling, calling you a fraud. What on earth was it about?"

Her personable routine always rubbed Lacey the wrong way. Lacey knew Taryn wasn't here because she cared. She was here for the gossip, which she could then spread around town.

"It was just a misunderstanding," Lacey replied dismissively.

"But why was there a man in the street in his pajamas?" Taryn asked, acting as if they were all great friends and she wasn't getting malevolent glee from this. "Saying he's going to ruin you? And telling everyone not to shop in your store?"

Lacey's mouth dropped open. "He said what?"

"He was ranting and raving up and down the high street telling everyone you were a fraud," Taryn told her, more than happy to oblige.

Lacey sunk her head into her hands. That was not good. Beyond tarnishing her reputation among the horsey folk, he'd set the tongues of the Wilfordshire rumor mill wagging.

"I'm going to see Tom," Lacey said, standing.

The last thing she needed was to sit here and listen to Taryn recount the whole thing. She needed comfort.

The patisserie was, well, a bit of a mess. Tom clearly hadn't had a chance to clean down the tables in a while, as they were strewn with crumbs.

Lacey headed into the kitchen where she found him using an electric whisk to whisk batter in his left hand, while piping frosting onto muffins with his right hand. And she thought her day had been bad.

"You look like you need some help," Lacey said.

Tom startled at her voice and looked over. "Lacey," he said, managing to flash her a loving grin despite doing two other things at once. "Is the auction over?"

Lacey nodded. She collected the wipes and went out to clean all the tables. A moment later, Tom came out of the kitchen and wrapped his arms around her. "What happened?" he asked softly in her ear.

"What makes you think something happened?" she said stiffly.

"I can tell by your face."

Tom wasn't usually perceptive. Perhaps her words to him before had sunk in and he was really making an effort to prove to her how much he cared. Which only made her feel even worse about everything that had happened with Colin.

She sighed. "The auction went well. I sold tons. There was an argument at the end, but nothing I couldn't handle."

"Then why so glum?" Tom asked tenderly, tipping her chin up with his fingertips so their eyes met.

It was on the tip of her tongue, the whole situation with Colin, when the patisserie's phone started ringing.

Tom pulled a strained face. "Damn. I'm sorry. I'm expecting a call. I really need to take it."

"Take it," Lacey said, shaking her head.

There was no point hanging around here if Tom wasn't even able to give her half his attention, so she went back to her store. It was now completely empty. Lacey had gone from having a packed store to having a completely empty one.

"Lacey?" she heard someone say from behind.

She turned. It was Carol, the B&B owner.

"I heard about your auction," she said. "Are you okay?"

Typical. The gossip was already spreading.

"I'm fine," Lacey told her.

Gina bustled toward them. "Sorry, Carol, we have loads to tidy up, do you mind coming back later?" She shooed the nosy woman right out into the street, then turned back to Lacey. "You need to go home."

"No I don't," Lacey countered.

"Yes. You do. You've had a crazy day. You'll be out of adrenaline soon, and then you'll crash. I'd prefer you to crash at home than here. I'm not in the mood to scoop you up off the floor like a puddle."

She was exaggerating, of course, but Lacey relented. "Thanks, Gina. As long as you're sure?"

"I'm sure. Go. Get some sleep. I'll see you tomorrow."

Lacey did as her surrogate mother commanded.

She made it back to Crag Cottage and face planted onto her bed.

⚜ ⚜ ⚜

*Ring-ring. Ring-ring.*

Lacey darted her head up. She was shocked to find herself lying prone on her bed, in her clothes from yesterday. Sunlight was streaming in through the window. It was morning.

"I slept through the night!" she exclaimed.

Gina was right about her crashing.

*Ring-ring. Ring-ring.*

Bleary eyed, Lacey grabbed her cell off the bedside table and answered.

"Yes?" she croaked.

"Lacey, this is really interesting," came an unfamiliar voice.

"Who is this?"

"Gabe."

"Gabe?" She'd never heard the boy sound anything but grumpy or nonchalant. But now he sounded positively animated. "What is? What's interesting?"

"The report. From your network provider. About the lag in your connection during the auction."

Reports, networks, and connections weren't exactly "interesting" to Lacey. They were especially less so when her head was still foggy from sleep.

"Go on."

"There wasn't just a lag, there was an interruption. Like a router being reset or a modem unplugged."

"I don't get it. What does that mean?"

"It could just be a glitch. Or it could mean someone deliberately interfered with the auction."

Lacey sat up straight, now completely awake. "You mean like sabotage?"

"I wouldn't want to jump to any conclusions," Gabe said, sounding distinctly like he was about to jump to a conclusion. "But yeah."

After the call, Lacey pondered it further, and remembered the way Oxana had bid just one pound more. She'd thought she was being petty at the time, putting in a jab just before bowing out, but now she wondered if there'd been more to it. A hustle. Could she have gotten someone else to cut the connection?

Whatever had happened, Lacey wanted to get to the bottom of it. She had a full-blown mystery on her hands, and she hadn't even gotten out of bed yet!

She spent her morning shower pondering the so-called glitch. Then she spent her morning coffee pondering it. By the time she was ready to take Chester on his beach walk, she'd made a decision. If Oxana had done something untoward to win the sculpture, then she'd have to get the police involved, and it would nullify the sale. So before she accused anyone of anything, she'd like to know if Hugh Buckingham would still be willing to match his original bid. Which meant apologizing...

She shuddered at the thought. Hugh had been a particularly unpleasant individual to deal with. Not to mention he seemed super sick and a dose of summer flu was the last thing Lacey needed right now. But she didn't want to miss out doubly. If the sculpture wasn't sold now, she'd have to wait a whole year before the horsey crowd rolled into town again.

She reached Gina's back door and knocked.

Her neighbor answered, already suited and booted and ready to go. Boudica bounded out, clearly excited for her morning walkies. They headed down the cliffs together and on to the beach.

It was a beautiful morning, and the beach was packed with horsey people.

"I had an interesting call this morning," Lacey told Gina. "From Gabe."

"You meant to say he actually strung a sentence together?" Gina quipped.

"He did." She cast her mind back to the groggy early morning call. "He was quite animated, actually. Apparently Hugh might've had a point. The internet *was* cut during the Isidore Bonheur sale."

"Really?" Gina exclaimed. "Deliberately?"

"There's no way of knowing," Lacey said. "But my hunch is that Oxana had a hand in it."

"What are you going to do?"

"I need to see if Hugh still wants to buy the statue. I'm going to see if I can talk to him, face to face."

"Is that sensible?" Gina asked. "Hugh was like a powder keg ready to explode. Don't be the spark."

It was a good point. Maybe Lacey was meddling more than she ought to.

But when they reached the store and Lacey unlocked it, the place remained empty. Hugh's angry diatribe had driven off the customers.

Lacey rifled through her records, finding Hugh's contact details from the list of virtual attendees.

"Tolleton Green?" she said aloud, immediately recognizing the name of the town. It was the posh one just north of Wilfordshire, the one where Suzy was from. Where Gabe was from as well, since he was her neighbor.

She was surprised to see Hugh lived so close by. His sickness had prevented him from attending the auction in person. If he'd been there, Lacey wouldn't be in this mess in the first place. It seemed so unfair for him to miss out on the sale because of a technical glitch.

She made up her mind.

"Chester," she said. "Let's go and see Hugh."

Gina rolled her eyes, clearly unhappy with the decision Lacey had made, but she ignored her, jumped in her car, and maneuvered her way out of the busy streets of Wilfordshire.

Tolleton Green was a quaint place, where there were more fields than houses, the houses looked like castles, and all the front lawns were as big as parks. Everything seemed perfectly maintained, from the tidy hedges to the immaculately maintained flowerpots, and the neat, sweeping drive-ways that each had several expensive-looking cars parked along them.

As she passed trees teeming with sparrows and thrushes, Lacey wondered whether she was doing the right thing or not. If Hugh was still willing to match his original bid, how would she then go about getting the statue back off Oxana? The businesswoman didn't seem like the sort who'd willingly hand it back, and she certainly didn't seem like she'd give up without a fight. Was Lacey stoking the flames by giving Hugh an inch?

"We're looking for Hyacinth House," Lacey told Chester, because of course none of the houses had street numbers.

She drove to a crawl, peering at all the signs at the bottom of the driveways. Charingworth House. Paeonies. And then...

"There! Hyacinth House."

Lacey turned onto the long paved driveway and approached the house, where there was a cream Rolls Royce parked outside.

Lacey parked (not too close, just in case), and went up to the front door with Chester by her side. She rang the bell and listened to its chime echoing on the other side. She couldn't hear anyone inside.

Just then, Chester started whining and scratching at the door.

"Hey, boy, stop that," Lacey said. "What's the matter?"

But he kept on whining.

Lacey hadn't seen him behave like that before. He seemed so fraught, Lacey decided to try the handle, just to test whether it was locked or not. She heard the latch click open as she pressed on it.

She hadn't been planning on barging into Hugh's home but Chester was giving her the heebie-jeebies, so she did.

She gave the door a push, feeling heavy resistance from the other side. She pushed a little harder and heard something moving. Whatever was behind the door had been shifted slightly. Now that the door was open a crack, Chester's barks became more insistent and frantic. Lacey shoved with all her weight and the resistance on the other side gave. Something large, dark, and heavy slumped to the side.

Lacey screeched as she realized she was looking at Hugh Buckingham, slumped sideways on the floor. He was dead.

# Chapter Sixteen

Fighting her instinct to run, Lacey crouched down beside the slumped figure. She felt compelled to double-check whether Hugh really was dead. What if he'd just passed out? He'd obviously been extremely unwell when she'd last seen him in her store.

She pressed her trembling fingers to Hugh's neck, hoping to find even the smallest flutter of a pulse. But there was nothing there. Hugh Buckingham's skin was cold to the touch. He was dead.

"Chester! Get back!" Lacey exclaimed, overcome with shock and panic that she had, once again, stumbled upon a dead body.

As she hurried out the open front door, her hand went to her cell phone, and she called a number she wished she didn't have in her regularly dialed tab: the Wilfordshire Police. There was no point dialing the emergency 999; may as well go directly to the source.

"You're going to want to send someone down to Hyacinth House in Tolleton Green," she said, when the call connected. "A man has passed away."

"Is he conscious?" asked the officer on reception, a female with a slightly nasally voice that Lacey had met on occasion. Jacqui was her name, if Lacey recalled correctly.

"No."

"Breathing?"

"No," Lacey repeated. "He's passed. I'm sure of it."

"Do you know how to do CPR?"

Lacey knew these were standard questions in this situation, but she also knew in Hugh's case it would be entirely pointless; he was quite clearly long dead. The last thing she wanted to do was get her DNA all over him. She still had no idea what had happened to cause his demise.

"I'm pretty sure it's too late for that," Lacey said.

Jacqui paused. She was probably making a record of this. That the caller had refused to administer CPR. If something untoward had happened to cause Hugh's death, then her refusal would be a big red mark against her name. The second, in fact, because the first was of course the fact she was the first to discover the body. Hopefully there'd be an innocent explanation for Hugh's death, that it was natural causes, and this would all blow over quickly. But Lacey also knew that life never seemed to go smoothly for her, and it would be just her bad luck that it wasn't.

"What's your relation to the deceased?" Jacqui asked.

Lacey paused. Jacqui was veering off script. Clearly, she already thought there may be more going on here.

Lacey chose her words carefully. "I know him in a professional capacity."

"You work together?"

"I'm an auctioneer. He was a customer."

A beat of silence passed. Then the nasally officer asked, "Lacey? Is that you?"

Lacey's shoulders slumped. Being identified on first-name terms by the local police station wasn't exactly something to be proud of.

"Yes," she said stiffly.

"Okay, stay where you are," Jacqui replied. "I've passed the information on to the emergency services in Tolleton Bay. But between you and me, DOAs always go to the bottom of the list. It might be a little while before anyone reaches you. Can you stay until the officers get there?"

"Of course," Lacey replied, though in the back of her mind she was wondering how much of Jacqui's request was due to suspicion. The female officer had seen Lacey in the Wilfordshire police station often enough, after all, and depending on whether she was closer to Beth Lewis or Karl Turner probably determined how much prejudice she harbored against the outsider who always found herself in sticky situations.

"Do you know if the premises are secure?" Jacqui continued. "Any sign of an intruder? Broken doors, windows, that sort of thing?"

Lacey stepped back from the welcome mat on the porch and gazed across the front of the house. Everything looked perfectly fine from the outside. "Nothing I can see," she told her.

"And can you confirm to me you don't have any weapons on you?"

"Me?" Lacey asked, surprised. She knew it was part of the script Jacqui had to follow to keep everyone safe, but it still felt like an accusation. "No. Not at all."

There was a pause. "And your dog?"

"Chester. Yes. He's here."

"Might want to put him on a leash."

"My dog isn't a weapon," Lacey replied, tersely.

"The Tolleton police don't know that," Jacqui said simply. "I'm just making sure everyone is safe and the situation doesn't escalate."

"Fine," Lacey replied.

She reached into her coat pocket for the leash. But it was empty. Chester's leash was no longer there.

Lacey's heart dropped as she looked through the open front door of Hyacinth House. The leash was lying on the marbled floor. It must have fallen from her pocket in her haste to get out.

In her ear, Jacqui was still talking, explaining how she was going to pass the case information on to Superintendent Turner, but Lacey was only half listening now. She was busy wondering if she should risk heading back into the house to retrieve Chester's leash, or if it would be worse for her just to leave it there. If Superintendent Turner arrived before the Tolleton Green police did and saw the leash, would it give him ammunition against her, and set him once again down the wrong path of suspicion?

"Are you still there, Lacey?" came Jacqui's voice.

"Yes," Lacey replied, her eyes fixed firmly on the leash. "Sorry. What did you say?"

"I said I was right about Superintendent Turner wanting to take a look at the scene. He's on his way to you now."

The call ended and Lacey's mind was made up. She'd have to reenter Hyacinth House to fetch the leash.

She stashed her phone in her pocket and steeled herself. Entering the house of a dead man was a terrible idea, not just because of accidentally shedding DNA over the scene, but also psychologically. It had taken her a long time to overcome the shock of Iris Archer's killing, and longer still to get the image of Buck out of her mind. She still thought about Wilfordshire's mayor lying face down on the drawing room floor of the Lodge, and Desmond's unseeing eyes as she turned him in his armchair to face her. The last thing she really wanted to do was add another shudder-inducing memory to the vault.

But somehow, she found her resolve and stepped inside.

Chester, who usually followed her everywhere, stayed out on the porch, watching through the open door. Even her dog knew this was a terrible idea.

Striding toward the leash, Lacey became suddenly aware of just how cold Hugh Buckingham's house was. It felt like someone had the AC set all the way up to "igloo."

She grabbed the leash and turned back, her gaze immediately drawn to the deceased man.

Noting Hugh's position by the door, half slumped against a potted plant, Lacey couldn't help her curiosity. How had he died? There was no sign of foul play. No obvious injuries. No bruises, scrapes, or blows. No signs of a struggle. It was as if Hugh Buckingham had simply keeled over and died.

She wondered whether he'd been on his way in, or on his way out when it happened. He was dressed in his night robe, which in a normal circumstance Lacey would assume meant he was heading out rather than in—to fetch a paper or answer the door, for example—but considering he'd appeared at her auction in the same attire meant all bets were off. If he'd been heading out, it might be because he was trying to escape something. Or someone. But that was all just wild speculation. Whether he was coming in or going out, either way he'd died right there by his front door, in the curiously frigid hallway of his multimillion-pound mansion.

Lacey scanned the hallways, looking to see if anything struck her as unusual. Nothing was in disarray at all. In fact, the whole place was pristinely clean.

There was nothing amiss, so Lacey turned to leave. But as she did, her focus was drawn to the large succulent plant Hugh was leaning into, his arm half-cocked against the rim of the heavy terracotta pot. His position reminded her a little of the drunk horsey folk weaving around the high street arm in arm, almost as if he'd been using the potted plant to hold himself up. Or pull himself up?

Lacey's focus was drawn then to the window panel behind the succulent. There was a window on either side of the door, a matching potted succulent placed in front of each, set up to be identical mirror images. But something was immediately different, like some kind of Spot the Difference puzzle. Condensation had formed on the windows, and above the top of the succulent beside the right-hand window, a smudge on the glass had emerged. A smudge that looked to have been very deliberately made by a finger. Tom had taught her the trick, by leaving a finger-drawn heart on her bathroom mirror so she'd see it once she stepped out of her steamy morning shower. The same thing had happened here. Someone's fingertip had marked the window with an X. And Lacey was quite certain that someone was Hugh.

The mark was just within reach of his right hand, if he'd drawn it across his body and reached up to where his left ear had now slumped, but where before would have been the space above his shoulder. There was no other explanation for how the mark could've gotten there, since that part of the window would usually be obstructed by the plant. But what did it mean? Was it just made in Hugh's last desperate, flailing attempt to stand, or was he leaving a message?

Lacey stepped closer to get a better look. Right beside the first X, there was another, slightly smaller and less well defined, but unmistakably there.

XX? What could it mean? Lacey's mind began ticking over.

Extra-large? X-rated? Initials?

Just then, Chester barked. Lacey glanced up and saw through the windows the police cruiser coming up the driveway.

She hurried out of the house in the nick of time and clipped on Chester's leash.

Lacey watched the cruiser taking its time to proceed up the long driveway, her anxiety increasing with each slow rotation of its tires on the gravel.

Finally, it ground to a halt and the stocky figure of Superintendent Turner emerged from the passenger side of the vehicle. DCI Lewis exited from the driver's side, her dark blonde hair pulled back into a ballerina-style bun. She gave Lacey a warm nod, in complete contrast to her male partner, who merely glowered.

"Lacey," Superintendent Turner said, dryly. "What a surprise."

Lacey immediately bristled. "Detectives."

"Tell me what happened here?" Superintendent Turner asked, pointing at the front door, which was standing ajar and letting out a steady stream of arctic air.

"I found him dead," Lacey said. "I think he was slumped against the door, but slid to the side when I pushed it open."

"You knew him personally?" Superintendent Turner asked, as he crouched down and peered through the gap in the door.

"He was a customer," Lacey said. "I was here to discuss an auction issue."

From his crouched position, Superintendent Turner looked over his shoulder and narrowed his eyes at her. "Do you usually walk straight into your customers' homes without waiting for them to answer the door?"

"I don't make a habit of it," Lacey said tersely.

Chester, picking up on the growing tension, began to growl. Superintendent Turner's eyes slid over to the dog.

"I remember now. It's Lassie who finds the bodies."

He sounded suspicious, but since he hadn't asked a direct question, Lacey said nothing.

Superintendent Turner switched his attention to DCI Lewis. "He's dressed in his bathrobe," he commented. The woman began to take notes. "And the heating is down low." He sniffed. "Olbas oil. So he was sick. Possibly more sick than he realized. Died of the flu."

Lacey wasn't so sure the man's death was natural once the circumstances surrounding it were factored in: a verbal altercation the day before his death (a very public, heated one); being in competition for an expensive antique and missing out because of a technical glitch and one single pound. Then there was the strange mark on the window. Maybe one X would have been easier to dismiss as nothing. But two? Two distinct marks? Lacey didn't think so. It seemed too much to her like Hugh's last desperate bid to communicate something.

She glanced again at the frosted glass window but realized she could no longer see the marks. Whether that was because they weren't visible through the frosted glass from the outside, or because they'd now faded, Lacey couldn't be sure. Maybe the temperatures between the outside and inside had now reached an equilibrium, rendering the marks invisible. Or maybe, Lacey considered, she'd just imagined them in the first place. Maybe Hugh really had just died of the flu and the antique statue had nothing to do with anything.

But in her heart, Lacey suspected she just wouldn't be so lucky.

# CHAPTER SEVENTEEN

A dead body. A talk with the cops. It wasn't exactly how Lacey had hoped her day would start.

She drove on autopilot back to Wilfordshire, so wrapped up in her thoughts she didn't even hear her cell phone ringing, nor Chester's secondary bark alert system. It was only after she'd found herself suddenly parked around the side of the store that she realized she'd missed several calls from Suzy—some from her personal cell number, some from the Lodge.

The thought of listening to the bright and cheery voice of her friend right now didn't appeal, so Lacey decided to defer calling her back until the evening.

Heavy-hearted, she got out of the car and headed back inside her store with Chester at her heels.

As she entered, the jolly tinkle of the bell seemed to be mocking her. The happy customers cooing at her vintage stock felt intrusive. Normally she'd be happy to have customers in the store but right now, all Lacey wanted to do was lock herself in her dark back office and block out the world. She needed some peace and quiet. Some cold air. She could feel a stress headache coming on.

Gina set upon her the moment she noticed her crossing the shop floor toward the back rooms.

"What is going on, Lacey?" she demanded, abandoning the customer she'd been chatting with and following her as she continued heading for the back room. "Where have you been? What makes you think it's okay to just leave me here to manage the store alone? Suzy's been trying to get hold of you, as well, though she wouldn't tell me why. Lacey. Lacey, are you even listening to me?"

Lacey halted and turned on her heel. She rubbed the deep furrow that had formed between her brows. "Can you just give me one second? Please," she said testily. "I have a pounding headache."

Gina softened immediately. "You don't look so great, dear. Has something happened?"

Lacey faltered. She couldn't exactly tell Gina she'd found a dead body with all these people in the store watching them. Hugh had already started the rumor mill's motors; the last thing Lacey wanted was to get it churning. It would eventually, she knew that. But if she could delay it for as long as possible, she would.

"I'll explain everything later," she told her friend. "Just give me five minutes, okay?"

Gina looked worried. But before Lacey had a chance to retreat to the privacy of her office, the door was pushed open with such force it bounced off the wall stopper. The bell let out an angry jangle, making every customer in the store turn their head.

In marched Oxana.

*There goes my peace and quiet,* Lacey thought wearily.

The snappily dressed businesswoman stopped at the counter, her lips pinched into a look of disgust.

"Give me the address of Hugh Buckingham," she demanded in her loud Ukrainian accent. Her aggressive tone was enough to make every single person in the store stop what they were doing and pay attention, dividing the store immediately into tourists and out-of-towners who stared, and discreet Brits pretending they were suddenly extremely interested in whatever piece of antique pottery they were holding while watching the unfolding scene out of the corner of their eye.

"I'm afraid I can't do that," Lacey said. "What do you even need it for?"

"He is a thief," Oxana declared. "He stole my statue." She drummed each word onto the countertop with her fingertip.

"The Isidore Bonheur?" Lacey exclaimed. The thought of a thief taking off with the precious antique statue filled her with revulsion. "It's been stolen?"

"Yes," Oxana replied brusquely. "By that snotty man Hugh Buckingham!"

Lacey frowned. She exchanged a skeptical glance with Gina. Something here stunk and she could tell from her friend's dubious expression she was thinking so too.

"Are you sure it was him?" Lacey asked.

"Who else would it be?" Oxana screeched. "That sweaty oaf came to my hotel and stole it right out of my room while I was sleeping!"

"The Lodge," Gina said, looking over at Lacey with sudden realization. "That must've been what Suzy was calling about."

Lacey nodded in agreement. Oxana was a guest at the Lodge; Suzy must've been trying to give Lacey a heads-up that she was on her way over. That'd teach her not to call her friends back.

Lacey was still unconvinced by Oxana's accusation. Dead men weren't particularly known for breaking into hotel rooms and stealing statues after all.

"What makes you think it was Hugh?" she questioned Oxana. "If you were asleep when it happened ... "

Oxana scoffed. "You saw how he acted at the auction! His hissy fit at being beaten by a woman. He is a brute. The sort of man that doesn't accept defeat. Especially not from a woman. You saw it with your own eyes, did you not?"

Her beady eyes went from Lacey to Gina and back again, shooting accusations from them like laser beams.

Lacey had indeed been on the receiving end of Hugh's angry cry of vengeance. He was a brute, that much was true. But a thief?

"Do you have any evidence, though?" Lacey pressed Oxana. "A witness? A clue?"

Oxana let out a sneer of mocking laughter, like a bark. "What is this? Are you Miss Marple?"

She looked around at her audience as if for approval. Thankfully, most of them were politely averting their eyes and pretending nothing was happening, a peculiarly British behavior Lacey had witnessed more than once since moving here.

Oxana looked back at Lacey. "No, Miss Marple, I have not got a witness! And sadly, he did not leave his calling card." She scoffed again. "But it was him and I am sure of it. So give me his address." She held her hand out, palm up.

"Now look here," Gina began, but Lacey held her arm out to hold her back. Gina wading in wasn't going to help this situation one bit. She had much more faith in her own ability to defuse the situation. As much as she loved Gina, and was touched that her friend wanted to stand up for her, this was something she'd prefer to handle on her own.

Gina got the hint. She buttoned her lips and folded her arms, adopting the position of a silent supporter.

Lacey took over. She shook her head at Oxana. "I can't give you that information."

"Why?" Oxana said accusatorily. "Because you are afraid of breaking a rule?"

She was half right. Lacey couldn't legally give her his address. But she also couldn't because ... well, because Hugh was lying dead on his hallway floor.

"Pretty much," Lacey said.

"This," Oxana declared, "is why I am Ukraine's wealthiest female CEO of an industrial company and why you are just a silly little shop lady!"

Lacey's jaw dropped open. Gina's ability to stay quiet failed.

"Now listen!" she exclaimed.

But her retorts were drowned out by Oxana's extremely loud voice, which was so domineering and commanding, it sent most of the people in the store scurrying for the exit.

"You will never get anywhere in life by being a good little girl!" the woman ranted. "By following the rules! Do you think men like Hugh got where they were by being obedient? No! They got there by bullying! By stealing!"

She was getting rather riled now, and Lacey's confidence in defusing the situation faltered.

"If you will not help me," Oxana shouted with finality, "then I will call the police!"

"Good idea," Lacey said. It was what she should've done in the first place.

But when Lacey realized Oxana was calling them to the store, her heart sank. The last thing she wanted right now was to speak to the cops again!

"Won't they want to speak to you back at the Lodge?" Lacey suggested to Oxana. "Since that's where the crime happened?"

"No," the woman replied bluntly, her cell phone up to her ear. "You are not going to shoo me away. They will come here and talk to me here."

Lacey sank into the stool and dropped her head into her hands. Her day was going from bad to worse.

Superintendent Turner arrived with a look of malevolent triumph on his face. He marched into Lacey's store—now devoid of customers, thanks to Oxana's continued tirade—looking like the cat who'd gotten the cream.

"Hello again," he said in his stiff, unpleasant way. "I was just saying to Lewis how the only thing that would make this day better was running into you for a second time."

Lacey didn't rise to his antagonistic sarcasm, and DCI Beth Lewis looked thoroughly unimpressed by him.

"Sarge, please," she said.

Lacey smiled. It was good to see Beth Lewis standing up to him, even if only a little.

Oxana paced toward them, her hands on her hips. "Are you here about Hugh Buckingham?" she said.

Lacey tensed. Both detectives snapped their faces toward her. They were wearing twin expressions of confusion.

"We're here regarding a theft," Superintendent Turner said, his eyes narrowing at Lacey before finally turning back to Oxana. "What made you bring up the name Hugh Buckingham?"

DCI Lewis hastily removed her notebook from her breast pocket and clicked the top of her pen, looking expectantly at Oxana.

"I beat him during the auction," Oxana said, waving her hand theatrically as if reveling in their undivided attention. "He was furious. And now the item has been stolen! Any intelligent person can put two and two together. Who else would it be?"

"How interesting…" Superintendent Turner said, his stone cold glare flicking back to Lacey.

*Perfect,* Lacey thought. A connection had been made between a dead man and her antiques store. That wouldn't look good for her.

"Lewis," Superintendent Turner commanded. "Take down Mrs.…"

"Kovalenko," Oxana said. "And it's Ms." She flashed him a sultry smile.

Superintendent Turner looked indifferent. "…Kovalenko's statement," he finished saying to Beth. "I need a word with Lacey."

DCI Lewis nodded. She took the businesswoman to one side.

Superintendent Turner faced Lacey. "Why is it," he said, taking a slow step toward her, as if relishing the moment, "that whenever something happens in this town, *you're* involved?"

"Coincidence?" Lacey offered. It wasn't the wisest move to make, antagonizing Superintendent Turner like that, but the man got right under her skin and, after the day she'd had, she just couldn't help herself.

From where DCI Lewis was taking down Oxana's statement, she craned to look over her shoulder, watching like a hawk as her so-called superior harassed a witness.

"Tell me about this item," Superintendent Turner said, leaning his elbow on the counter.

"What do you want to know?" Lacey said, coolly. "It was a bronze jockey statue? Made by Isidore Bonheur? One of France's finest animalier sculptors? Produced circa 1800? Is that enough information or do you need to know more?"

Beside her, Gina let out a snort of amusement.

"How about its price?" Superintendent Turner replied, bullishly.

Lacey pursed her lips. "Is that relevant?"

"Could be."

Lacey logged into her computer and pulled the information up. "It sold for five thousand and one pounds."

"And one pound? Is that usual?"

Lacey shrugged. "Depends on the situation. It was a hard battle between two bidders. One of them pushed the bid up by a pound, then won." She

avoided eye contact with Oxana. She didn't want the fierce woman to realize just how petty she thought the whole thing had been. Nor get any incli-
nation that she was suspicious that she may have only put in the one-pound
increase because she knew the online system would cut out and she'd win.

Superintendent Turner said nothing more on the topic. "Can we do a
sweep of your store?"

"Here?" Lacey said. "Why? Wouldn't it make more sense to focus
your efforts on the Lodge?"

Superintendent Turner narrowed his eyes. "I don't need you to tell
me how to do my job, thank you very much," he said in a clipped tone.

Lacey let out a weary sigh. "Fine. Whatever. Be my guest." As much
as she loathed the police rummaging around in her business where they
weren't wanted, it wasn't like she had anything to hide, and any protesta-
tion on her part would just prolong the situation.

As Superintendent Turner and DCI Lewis began their search, Gina
flashed Lacey a sympathetic look and gave her arm a reassuring squeeze.
It was probably her way of apologizing for biting her head off earlier.
Lacey accepted the gesture with a weary smile.

Superintendent Turner and DCI Lewis returned.

"Well?" Oxana asked, brusquely.

"Nothing of note," DCI Lewis confirmed, her tone implying
Superintendent Turner's decision to search the antiques store had been
the wrong call.

Lacey held back a smirk of vindication.

Superintendent Turner looked at Oxana. "We'll need to take a look at
the scene," he told her. "Will you accompany us to the Lodge?"

"Yes," the woman said with a huff, turning on her heel and marching
away.

Lacey followed her and the detectives to the door.

"Don't take any impromptu trips out of town," Superintendent Turner
muttered as he exited.

"I wouldn't dream of it," Lacey replied wryly.

She shut the door behind them and watched the cruiser drive away.
Then she locked the door and turned the sign over. She'd had about
enough of the world as she could take for one day.

# CHAPTER EIGHTEEN

E vening fell on a curiously quiet day at the store. Lacey was dusting the shelves when she felt her phone vibrating in her pocket.

She retrieved it and saw an unrecognized number on the screen. Probably a cold caller. She answered anyway, just in case it was important.

"Lacey?" the voice said on the other end. "It's Beth. DCI Lewis."

"Beth?" Lacey echoed. Why was the detective calling her? "Is this your personal phone?"

She headed to the back room for some privacy.

"Yes. I wanted to let you know there's been a development in Hugh's case."

"Oh?"

"The preliminary autopsy report just came back. It's stated the mechanism as homicide."

Lacey paused. "Hugh was murdered?"

"Yes. Toxicology is doing a full work-up now."

Beth didn't have to say what that meant, because Lacey knew full well why toxicology was getting involved. Hugh was poisoned.

Stunned, Lacey sank into her seat. For some reason, the idea that his death was caused by poisoning seemed far worse to her than if someone had killed him in a fit of passion, because it required a degree of forward planning, of meticulous scheming. It had to be someone close to Hugh as well, someone he trusted not to give him a drink or food laced with poison. The thought was too awful for Lacey to entertain.

Then another thought struck her. Why was Detective Lewis telling her this? Why had she called her in the first place?

A horrible thought dawned on Lacey. "Is Superintendent Turner making me a suspect?" she asked, already knowing the answer.

There was hesitation from Beth's end of the line. "Yes," she finally admitted. "I'm sorry, Lacey, he is."

Both women knew it was stupid. They'd been through this enough now for DCI Lewis to know Lacey wasn't a killer. But her male counterpart stubbornly refused to see things that way. When it came to Lacey, he was as blinkered as a horse at the races.

"That's why I wanted you to hear it from me first," Beth continued.

Lacey couldn't imagine the amount of procedural rules she'd circumvented to give her this warning. She greatly appreciated that at least one of the detectives was smart and fair.

"Can you go through what happened in the shop for me again?" DCI Lewis asked. "I know you already gave your statement, but I think it would be helpful for me to hear it firsthand."

Lacey could read between the lines. DCI Lewis didn't trust her superior not to have missed a crucial bit of information from her original statement.

"I was in the back office," Lacey said, recalling how she'd not been alone, because Colin had come in and tried to kiss her. She decided that bit wasn't relevant. "Gina was out front. I heard the shouting and the dogs started barking so I hurried to see what was going on, and found him there in a bathrobe and slippers. He'd must've driven here the minute I sold the statue to Oxana because it was barely ten minutes after the end of the auction when he arrived."

"How did he look?"

"Extremely unwell. Feverish. Sweaty." Lacey winced, realizing how much he must have been suffering in that moment from the effects of poisoning.

"Will your CCTV back up that he was sick when he arrived?"

"It's black-and-white," Lacey explained. "I doubt you'll be able to see how sick he is on it."

"That's a shame," Lewis said. "Were there witnesses? We have dozens from outside the store but they were all drunk so considered unreliable. But if there was anyone independent from inside who could corroborate that would be really useful."

"And by independent, what do you mean?" Lacey queried.

"As in not a friend or colleague. Turner won't discount you as a suspect if the only witnesses are close to you."

Beyond her and Gina there was Colin. But he certainly didn't fit the criteria of "independent" considering their ... history.

"Oxana was there," Lacey said, clicking her fingers. "She was standing in the doorway watching the whole thing. She marched in and took the statue, then blew him a kiss."

"She blew him a kiss?" Beth repeated. "That's a bit odd, isn't it?"

"Yes. I thought so too."

Suddenly, Lacey was hit with a memory. The two X's she'd seen on the window. She'd gone through hundreds of different ideas for what they may have actually been. But she'd not considered one very significant thing an X signified. Kisses!

Had Hugh been trying to communicate that the woman who blew him a kiss had been the one to kill him?

"Lacey?" Beth Lewis's voice sounded in her ear. "Are you still there?"

"Yes," Lacey said breathlessly, gripping the phone tighter. "I was thinking of something. Back when I was at Hugh's house, I saw something on the window. It looked like someone had drawn an X. Two X's, actually. I thought it might've just been a smudge or something accidental before, but now I'm wondering if they were kisses, and they were put there on purpose."

"Interesting," DCI Lewis said. "I don't recall anything in the report about X's."

"That's the thing," Lacey added. "They were drawn in the condensation. It looked like they disappeared by the time the officers got there. I did mention it in my statement. I guess Turner didn't think it was relevant."

Beth was silent on the other end of the line, but Lacey could imagine her nostrils flaring with irritation. "Lacey, I'm doing everything I can to sort this out and clear you. But if there's anything else, no matter how irrelevant it might seem, can you let me know? Anything at all?"

Lacey thought of Colin. He'd witnessed the altercation, but he wouldn't count as independent in Superintendent Turner's eyes. What was the point of bringing it up and embarrassing herself? She'd just be making herself look bad for no reason.

"Nothing," she said.

"Okay. Because Karl's determined to get someone in custody before the full toxicology report comes back."

"How long will that be?"

"A few days."

Lacey's chest sunk. That didn't give her much time to clear her name. The stop-clock on her freedom was ticking.

"He can't arrest me on a hunch though, can he?" Lacey queried. "He needs at least some substantive evidence. What does he even have on me, beyond me being the one to find the body?"

"I'm sorry, Lacey. But I really shouldn't be discussing this with you."

"Now you want to stop talking to me about it?" Lacey challenged. "Come on, Beth. At least tell me what I'm up against here."

Beth exhaled. "Fine. Turner saw multiple phone calls on your records from the Lodge. The same location the statue was stolen from. He thinks someone there tipped you off about the statue, and that the theft and the murder are connected."

So Turner had incorrectly correlated Suzy's repeated calls with the stolen valuable antique. He'd put two and two together and come up with five.

Lacey slumped back in her chair, only half aware of Beth's voice as she bade farewell and hung up. She couldn't believe this was happening. The police were on her case again.

"Lacey?" came Gina's voice from the door.

Lacey swirled in her office chair. Gina had her shoulder up against the door frame.

"That was DCI Lewis," Lacey told her. "I'm a suspect."

"Oh." Gina's shoulders slumped. "What are you going to do?"

"I'm going to clear my name," Lacey said, determinedly. She grabbed a piece of paper from her desk, and a pen. "It's diagram time."

"Maybe I should buy you some red string and a chalkboard for your birthday," Gina joked, as Lacey began covering her paper with notes and arrows and circles, all connecting from one to the other.

Lacey shot her narrowed eyes. "This isn't a joking matter," she said.

Gina held her hands up in a truce. She was obviously just trying to lighten the mood, but Lacey wasn't up for it.

She looked back down at her notes. All arrows led back to one name. Oxana.

"Oxana won the statue," Gina said. "Why would she kill Hugh after winning?"

"Maybe he threatened her with legal action? He seemed to think that he'd won the item, after all, and he didn't seem like the most rational of humans either."

"Doesn't seem like enough to me," Gina said. "Are you sure you're not just targeting her because you don't like her?"

Lacey shook her head. She ringed the X in Oxana's name in red.

Gina narrowed her eyes. "What does that mean?"

"When I was at Hugh's house," Lacey explained, "I saw this mark on the window. Two X's."

"That could mean anything," Gina countered. "Or nothing at all."

"You're right. But I have nowhere else to look, so I may as well start there. There was obvious animosity between Oxana and Hugh. Oxana's name was spelled with an X. She blew him a kiss."

"Lacey, that sounds far-fetched," Gina told her.

"Maybe it is. But it's where I'm going to start." She swiped up her car keys from the counter and whistled to Chester. He leapt straight to attention, ready as ever to be the sidekick to Lacey's sleuth. They left the store side by side.

# Chapter Nineteen

The second Lacey emerged from her store onto the sidewalk the whispers started. A lot of the horsey folk were occupied today with a special race taking place at the tracks in the countryside out Penrose Manor way, so it was mainly locals milling around, speaking behind their hands to one another, pointing and gossiping. Lacey kept her chin up high, drawing strength from the trusty guard dog by her side.

She must have overheard the word "dead" and "statue" at least twenty times by the time she reached the end of the high street, where the Coach House Inn stood on the corner. Its doors were open today, thanks to the hot weather. The sounds of merriment from inside ebbed out.

Lacey glanced through the open door, noting that the place was packed to the rafters. Everyone was facing in the same direction, toward the large flat-screen TV mounted against the wall. The horse race taking place just a mile away was on the screen. Obviously the locals watched the show from the comfort of their favorite pub, rather than spend money on the extortionate ticket prices to attend in person like the tourists did.

Lacey picked a couple of familiar faces out of the crowd—Stephan, her landlord at the store, Jake, the volunteer lifeboat captain, Sakura, the pretty Japanese woman who owned Lacey's favorite sushi bar, and Brenda the big-mouthed barmaid with her brute of a boyfriend, Ed.

Then Lacey stopped, recalling Gina's words about how the horsey folk took over the Coach House during the festival, and were in there from dawn until dusk. Would she find Oxana inside?

Taking a chance, she entered in through the open doors, with Chester at her heels.

The Coach House Inn was stuffy inside, thanks to the weather and too many bodies packed into one place. The smell of stale beer was rather unpleasant, not to mention the slightly sticky floorboards. Chester kept close to Lacey's legs as she squeezed her way in through the throng.

Then suddenly, she saw her, sitting on a stool at the bar. Oxana.

*What a stroke of luck!* Lacey thought, as she wove through the wall of people toward the Ukrainian tycoon.

The woman seemed to be wobbly on her stool. By the looks of the empty champagne bottle on the bar beside her, and the red-lipstick-rimmed glass, she was well on her way to sozzle-town. It seemed pretty early to be drunk, Lacey thought.

She popped out of the crowd, bumping into Oxana's back as she did so. The woman turned fiercely. "Watch it," she growled in her harsh accent. Then, on recognizing who it was who'd bumped into her, added, "Oh. It's you." She couldn't have sounded less thrilled if she tried.

"You're not at the races," Lacey commented.

"No. I prefer to watch from here," Oxana said. "That way, when I win, I can buy everyone a round. That's what I did yesterday after winning the statue." She took a swig from her glass. "But that turned out to be premature, didn't it?"

She directed her accusation at Lacey. She clearly blamed her for the mix-up at the auction, and the subsequent theft of her statue.

"You came here last night?" Lacey asked.

"Didn't I just say that?" Oxana snapped.

She was a hostile drunk, Lacey noted. But if she was telling the truth, there'd be a whole load of witnesses. Depending on when Hugh died, Oxana may have an entire pub of alibis on her side.

"Was that when your statue was stolen?" Lacey asked. "When you were in here?"

"No. It was definitely there when I got back to my room. Hugh must've come in when I was passed out and taken it."

Lacey could just picture Oxana lying face down on her bed at the Lodge, stilettos still on, passed out from too much champagne. But she couldn't picture Hugh Buckingham sneaking in. Beyond the fact he was incredibly sick and lumbering, how would he have even known where to find her? He'd have to have watched her all evening until she returned to the B&B to even know where she was saying, and then how would he have gotten into her room? The Lodge was extremely secure. Suzy wasn't the type of proprietor to let strange men wander the hallways. That said, there was the drawing room bar that was open to the public, as well as the dining room, so if he'd been extremely sneaky, there was a slim chance he may have been able to pull it off.

But just how sneaky could a sick man really be?

There was one way to clear it up. Lacey needed to speak to Suzy. If Hugh had been witnessed at the Lodge that evening, then there was a high chance he was indeed the one to steal the statue. And if he had stolen the statue, had Oxana killed him to get it back?

Lacey drove to the Lodge and walked into the large, marble-floored foyer with the stone fountain in the center, then out into the corridor, where the large mahogany reception desk cleaved the hallway in two, separating the staff areas from the public areas. There was a girl on the reception desk Lacey hadn't seen before, looking bored and lost in her cell phone.

She remembered how Suzy had told her about her neighbor's kids staying with her and working. Maybe this was Gabe's sister, the college dropout? There was extra staff during the busy festival period. If only Tom had a neighbor with a couple of loafing young adults to send his way...

But then Lacey reminded herself that Tom didn't move in the same world as Suzy. As Hugh. The world of wealth. He didn't live in the affluent town of Tolleton Green, where the houses looked like mansions and the yards looked like parks. Tom didn't have a huge nest egg from his parents to pay wayward young people to do a semi-decent job. Everything he achieved, he did through sweat, grit, and sheer determination. It was one of the things she loved about him.

She walked over to the desk.

"Is Suzy here?" she asked the distracted-looking girl.

The receptionist looked up. She was young enough not to have any fine lines on her face, with the milky complexion of a model selling face cream. Her hair was highlighted and styled in pretty, soft waves. Her lips were rose pink. If she was Gabe's sister, she couldn't have been more different.

"No, I'm sorry, she's not," she said, in a floating, high-pitched voice. "Do you have a booking?"

Lacey stepped closer. "What about Lucia? Is she here?"

While Lacey still wasn't exactly close with Lucia after the whole debacle of the woman working with Tom, they were on friendly terms these days, and she knew she would help her if asked, and as the manager at the Lodge, she was perfectly placed to know the comings and goings.

The receptionist just shook her head. "No, sorry. It's just me." She smiled sweetly. "I like your dog."

"Thanks," Lacey said, looking down at the Border collie who was looking exceptionally cute as he waited patiently. She looked back at the receptionist, noting her delicate floral perfume. "Are you new here?"

The woman shook her head. "I'm just helping out. My parents sent me and my brother here for a week because they thought we needed to learn new life skills." She rolled her eyes. "As if I need life skills." She fluttered her long lashes at Lacey.

So she was Gabe's sister. And what an arrogant young woman, Lacey thought.

That put her at somewhere between nineteen and twenty-two, unless she dropped out of a post-grad degree. But by the way she chose to present herself—all pinks and blonde and flowery—Lacey couldn't really picture her as the academic type.

"You're Gabe's sister," Lacey said.

The girl looked surprised. "Oh. You know my smelly little brother, do you?"

"He did some work for me," Lacey explained.

She couldn't have looked more different from him. Where Gabe was scruffy and unkempt, his sister was polished to perfection. Perfectly manicured nails. Perfectly straight, whitened teeth. Where Gabe was a supposed genius on track to get a computer science degree, his sister seemed to be aspiring only to look pretty. The one thing they had in common was poor social skills.

"You must be Suzy's friend," the receptionist continued. "From the antiques store? I'm Emma."

"Nice to meet you," Lacey said. "I was wondering if you might be able to help me with something. Did you hear that one of the guests here reported a theft from their bedroom?"

"Yeah…" Emma said, looking distinctly uncomfortable at the change in direction the conversation had taken. "Suzy put me on the graveyard shift, and I was still there in the morning. I was the one who took the complaint."

Lacey tried to imagine this untrained young woman being barked at by the formidable Oxana. If her parents had sent her here for life experience, that was certainly a quick way of getting it!

"Were you on the desk when the complainant came in that evening?" Lacey asked.

"Yeah. She was steaming drunk. It wasn't even that late. Like seven or something like that."

"Was she alone?"

Emma nodded stiffly.

"Did you notice anyone hanging around who wasn't a guest? Specifically, a man in his fifties who looked unwell?"

Emma frowned and shrugged. "I don't even know all the staff, let alone the guests."

Interesting, Lacey thought. Had Emma unwittingly allowed Hugh Buckingham into the guests-only area of the Lodge, not realizing he shouldn't be there?

Lacey got out her phone and searched Hugh Buckingham's name. Men like him didn't get that rich without leaving a footprint. The first hit brought up a picture of the man, at least ten years younger but still recognizable enough. She turned the screen and showed it to Emma.

"This is the man."

The girl shifted uncomfortably. "I've never seen him before in my life," she said.

"Are you sure?" Lacey pressed. "He's a bit older than in that picture. He wasn't dining here? Or drinking in the drawing room?"

Emma shook her head. "Sorry, no."

She looked a bit distressed, and Lacey didn't want to put pressure on the poor girl. She put her phone away, satisfied that her suspicion had been confirmed: Hugh Buckingham wasn't the thief. Someone else had stolen the Isidore Bonheur sculpture from Oxana's room.

Just then, Emma's voice broke through Lacey's thoughts.

"There was this one guy, now I think of it," she said.

"Oh?" Lacey asked, her curiosity immediately piqued.

"He was in the drawing room for most of the evening. Just sitting there, looking a bit lost." She paused. " He seemed sad. I figured he'd been stood up, because it was just him and his dog."

"Dog?" Lacey asked.

Emma nodded. "Yes, it was a Border collie, just like yours."

Lacey felt the blood drain from her face. Colin.

# CHAPTER TWENTY

Lacey paced back and forth outside the Lodge, her mind flitting frantically through thoughts. Could Colin be the thief?

On the one hand, it made sense. He wanted the Isidore Bonheur. He'd missed out on it twice, so perhaps he'd grown frustrated and just taken it. He didn't seem like the stealing sort, but then again, Lacey didn't exactly know him well. He was able-bodied enough to commit the theft, and he'd been hanging around on the fringes this whole time. Though he'd come across as an honest guy when she'd spent time with him at Sawyer's—indeed, he'd let her win *twice*—did that really mean anything? If he'd stolen the statue, would he tell her? Lacey was sure the two events were connected somehow, and if Colin was the key to solving the theft, maybe that would help her solve the murder too.

Unless he himself was the murderer? She shouldn't be so quick to dismiss him as a suspect. It wouldn't be the first time she'd been fooled. And he had tried to kiss her. Maybe Hugh had witnessed it, and that was what his X's at the crime scene meant.

There was only one way to know for sure. She'd have to speak to Colin.

She swallowed hard and took out her cell phone. Colin had given her his number during their high tea in Weymouth, and she'd innocently programmed it into her phone. But that was before Gina told her off and accused her of "willful flirting," and before Colin had cornered her in her office and attempted to kiss her. Now it didn't look so innocent sitting in her phone, and dialing it was about as far from Lacey's wish of things to do than could be since she knew how it would look to him. But there was no other option. Emma had planted the seed of doubt in her mind, and now Lacey wouldn't be able to rest unless she cleared it up and investigated for herself.

"Wish me luck," she said to Chester as she hit the green dial button. He whined in sympathy.

Lacey felt her heart begin to race as she listened to the dial tone on the other end of the line, then the sound of the call connecting.

"Well, well, well," came the cheery voice of Colin. "If it isn't Lacey! I wasn't expecting to hear from you again."

Just from his voice, Lacey could tell he was grinning, and that she'd made his day by calling him. Too bad she was going to crush him when she revealed this wasn't a social call, but because she suspected him of being a thief, and possibly even a killer. But needs must.

"I was wondering if you wanted to meet for a coffee?" she said, feeling her pulse pounding in her ears.

"Really? I thought you'd never ask," Colin commented. "I'd love to. When are you free?"

"Now?" Lacey suggested, forcing a cordial voice through her clenched teeth.

On the other end of the line, Colin paused. Then he started to chuckle. "I can do now," he said, sounding thoroughly pleased with himself.

Lacey grimaced, just imagining his smarmy smile. She quickly wracked her brains for a suitable location to meet. The chances of her being seen by someone she knew on the main street or promenade was too high. Luckily, a few stores had recently opened up on a street that branched off the promenade road, probably thanks in part by the increased footfall from people staying at the Lodge and heading into town, and the small cafe beside the balloon store seemed a safer bet. "I know a cute little place off the beaten path. It's new. It's called Rosie's."

"Rosie's. Got it."

"I'll be there in five."

Lacey entered Rosie's to find Colin had beaten her to it. He was sitting at the window table, Stella asleep under the table beside his feet. The dog roused her sleepy head at the sound of Lacey's approach.

"You found the place okay?" Lacey asked nervously as she shucked off her jacket. "I know it's a little off the beaten track."

Colin stood and kissed her cheek. Lacey stiffened.

"It's just like the place we went to in Weymouth," he commented.

Lacey glanced around. He was right. It had similar floral curtains. The same style of white bistro tables. Colin probably thought she'd chosen it to make some kind of romantic gesture.

She slung her jacket over the back of the opposite seat and sat, grabbing the menu so she'd have something to look at other than Colin's penetrating gaze. She couldn't quite bring herself to look him in the eye, considering what he might have done.

"I'm guessing you heard the news about Hugh," Colin said, sounding straightforward and emotionless.

Lacey's gaze darted over the menu in surprise. Would a guilty person really bring up the topic of conversation immediately? Or was he bringing it up to give her a false sense of security?

"I did," she managed to say.

Colin let out a mournful sigh. "How are you coping?"

Lacey was a little surprised to hear someone be concerned for her well-being. Obviously she had no real connection to the victim, but the murder of anyone local caused shock waves. The people of Wilfordshire used gossip as a coping strategy, and since it was often directed at her, Lacey often found herself alone in her feelings. It felt nice to know someone actually cared.

"I'm okay," she confessed, feeling her defenses starting to drop. "A bit shaken. I was the one who found him."

"Oh goodness," Colin replied, sounding dumbfounded. "That's so dreadful. How come?"

"The mix-up over the auction," Lacey explained. "I thought there was a chance that Oxana had engineered the whole thing with the internet dropping out, and went over to see if he'd accept the bid amount he put in if I nullified her sale. Chester alerted me to him."

"Clever boy," Colin said, looking at the dog at her feet.

Just then, the waitress came over. She looked high school age to Lacey. She was probably earning a bit of summer holiday spending money.

She gave them a small, shy smile and tucked a strand of strawberry blond hair behind her ear. "Can I take your orders?"

Colin gestured to Lacey politely. She was just about to answer when her attention was diverted by someone passing by the window outside. She turned, and her eyes met none other than Tom's.

A bolt of shock went through her. What was he doing here, in this place off the main road? She'd specifically chosen it to avoid this situation!

Tom looked at her, his expression unreadable. Then he gave her a small wave, before jamming his hands in his pockets and striding away.

"Just a black Americano," Lacey said hypnotically, watching Tom's retreating figure through the window.

"Just an Americano?" Colin repeated in a jokey voice. "Is that all? Last date we had Dorset apple traybake and macchiatos."

"It wasn't a date," Lacey corrected. She couldn't stop herself. She felt mortified. Seeing Tom like that had rattled her. Suddenly, this didn't seem like a good idea at all.

Colin looked a little surprised by her interruption. The blonde waitress looked at her feet uncomfortably.

"Ah," he said, folding the menu and handing it back to the young waitress. He gave her a polite smile. "Make that two black Americanos."

The girl took his menu and shuffled away shyly.

The moment she was gone, Colin looked at Lacey, his head tipped to the side curiously. "So. What's this all about then? Since we're clearly not on a date."

"I'm seeing someone," Lacey blurted.

"Okay…" Colin replied. "And you invited me to coffee because…"

Lacey wracked her brains for a suitable excuse. "Because I wanted to talk to someone about Hugh."

Colin frowned. "And your *partner* isn't a suitable person to talk with?"

He looked put out. Lacey had to admit that was understandable. She'd thought she'd be able to keep up the ruse, but seeing Tom had changed her mind.

In response to Lacey's silence, Colin continued. "So I did misread the signals between us after all? In which case, I should apologize. It must have been wishful thinking on my part, to see chemistry when there was none."

His maturity took Lacey by surprise. She'd been expecting him to be rude about being led on. Instead, *he* was apologizing to *her*!

"You've nothing to apologize for," Lacey told him.

"Really?" Colin mused. "I tried to kiss a taken woman. I pursued her across Dorset, then followed her all the way to her auction."

Lacey was stunned. So Colin hadn't come to buy the statue? He'd come to see her?

"But you wanted it in Weymouth," she said. "We both ended up at the art store on the cherry tree street."

"I followed you," Colin replied. "I'd never even heard of Isidore Bonheur. I just wanted a reason to spend time with you."

Lacey was stunned. Colin hadn't stolen the statue—he didn't even care about it! All along, him hanging around the fringes had been about one thing, and one thing only. Her.

"Lacey?" Colin asked. "Are you okay?"

"Sorry. Yes. I … I just don't know what to say."

She was completely taken aback.

But more than just the efforts Colin had gone in his romantic pursuit of her was the fact he couldn't be the thief, because he'd just admitted he had no interest in the statue after all.

Unless he was lying to shed suspicion, of course. Though he seemed genuine, Lacey wasn't prepared to completely dismiss him.

# CHAPTER TWENTY ONE

After speaking with Colin, Lacey felt compelled to see Tom and explain everything that had been going on. It felt like a secret she was keeping from him, something shameful. She had not done anything wrong, indeed she would never do such a thing to Tom, but it felt that by not telling him she was making it somehow much worse.

She drove back to the store, parking in the side alleyway before crossing the street to the patisserie, Chester at her side.

She entered the store and looked over at the till. But instead of Tom, the till was being operated by a tall, dark-skinned young man with sparkling brown eyes.

Lacey was astonished. The stranger was wearing a uniform. He was clearly a new employee.

"Where is Tom?" she asked him, her eyes grazing over his name tag: Emmanuel.

"Mr. Forrester is on a break," Emmanuel told her politely, in a warm Kenyan accent.

"A break?" Lacey exclaimed. "Are you sure we're talking about the same Tom?" She couldn't remember the last time he'd taken a break.

Emmanuel chuckled. "Can I help at all? I've been trained on the coffee machine, and we have a selection of croissants, cakes, and sandwiches."

He was doing a good job, especially considering this was his first day. Possibly even his first hour.

Lacey shook her head. "No. I'm good, thanks. Can you tell Tom that Lacey stopped by?"

"Ah!" Emmanuel exclaimed with excitement. "You're Lacey? The Lacey?"

"The Lacey?" she replied, laughing. "That makes me sound like a celebrity. I'm Tom's girlfriend. Partner. Whatever you want to call it."

"But you look so young!" Emmanuel exclaimed.

It was an odd comment. Tom was only three years older than her, and had a pretty youthful way about him. It wasn't like there was an obviously huge difference between them. Maybe something had gotten a little lost in translation. Emmanuel was probably just trying to be nice.

"I'll take that as a compliment," Lacey said, a little bemused.

She headed out, wondering why Tom had failed to tell her he was hiring a new staff member. Sure, there was busy, but then there was just not being bothered enough to communicate. Had Tom gone off her?

As she crossed the bustling street, weaving her way through the crowds, her phone started to ring. Lacey grabbed it, hoping it was DCI Lewis telling her Turner had dropped his investigation into her. But instead, she saw it was her mom.

Lacey hesitated, not sure she was able to handle her mother right now, before hitting the green button.

"Mom? Is everything okay?"

"Yes, of course. I wanted to see what you wanted for your birthday."

Oh. That. It had slipped her mind. Or maybe she'd let it slip her mind because she didn't want it to happen.

"Nothing, Mom," Lacey said, as she shimmied around a group of men in suits drinking ale from glass tankards. "I'm a grown woman now. I don't need gifts."

"Tom said you'd say that."

Lacey frowned. "You've spoken to Tom?" She knew the two of them became bosom buddies on holiday, but it still seemed odd to her they were in telephone contact.

"Yes. I hear from him more often than I do my own daughter! I can't even remember the last time you called me."

"Why were you talking to Tom?" Lacey asked, ignoring her mom's woeful monologue. She was much more interested in what the two of them were discussing behind her back.

"Nothing," Shirley replied abruptly. "Just chitchat."

Lacey narrowed her eyes. She wasn't convinced. But it did make her feel better in a way. Tom wouldn't be making chitchat with his mom if he'd gone off her, would he? But then she remembered David's brunch dates with her mom and immediately scrapped that. Just because they were friendly, didn't mean he still cared.

"Mom, I need to go," Lacey said, finally having popped out of the crowd onto her side of the street. She noticed the donkey poster still stuck in her window. "If you want to do anything for me, you can make a donation to the local donkey sanctuary."

"Donkey sanctuary?" Shirley repeated, sounding completely bemused. "Honestly, Lacey, sometimes I feel like I hardly know who you are."

"Bye, Mom," Lacey said.

She headed into the antiques store. Chester hurried in first, rushing up to Boudica with so much excitement you'd think they'd not seen one another in days rather than hours.

But as the door closed behind Lacey, she realized she was standing in a deserted store. There wasn't a single customer perusing the shelves inside. Far from that first day when the rich horsey folk had almost entirely cleaned out her supply of retro lamps, the shelves were still brimming as if nothing had been touched all day.

"Because they haven't," Lacey said aloud, her shoulders slumping with the realization that news of Hugh's death must have reached the tourists. Of course they were now steering clear of her store. They must think she was involved.

"Gina?" Lacey called out, glumly. "Where are you?"

There was no answer. It was yet more evidence of the lack of customers. Gina didn't normally leave Boudica to keep an eye on things in the same way Lacey did with Chester. Boudica was less inclined to raise her head from her nap at the sound of the bell, making her a pretty bad bell.

Lacey went round the counter, noticing the light on her retro answering machine was blinking. She hit the button. The voice of a woman came out.

"My name is Ciara Oliviera. I recently attended your auction and won a pair of silver phoenix spurs. In light of what's happened, I've decided to pull out of the sale. I understand my ten percent down payment is non-refundable, and I will not be making the final ninety-percent payment installment."

Lacey dropped her head into her hands. Perfect. That was just what she needed; an empty shop and a lost sale.

But the machine wasn't done yet. The next message began. "This is Dustin Powell," a man's voice said. "I'm calling to cancel my order of military riding boots I won in your auction," and was swiftly followed by a lady, "Sabine Jardin, calling to cancel my order."

Cancel my order. Cancel my order. Lacey heard the same words over and over again, each one feeling more crushing than the last. The fact that the rich horsey people hadn't even come into the store to cancel in person spoke volumes—they were too scared to, and keeping a wide berth. Instead, her machine was full of cancelled orders. It was a disaster. Lacey had put so much money into that stock, and it had to sell specifically to this niche crowd. Any stock left over would sit for a whole year, losing her money.

Lacey jotted down each name, her heart pounding with disappointment. But as her list grew, her mind shifted gears, switching from focusing on herself and her auction back to Hugh's murder. What if one of these names she'd listed was the killer? Could someone else among the auction attendees be the thief and murderer? Perhaps someone who dropped out of the running for the Isidore Bonheur much sooner in the race than Hugh and Oxana, much sooner than Colin even?

Of course none of them followed the kiss theory, but maybe it didn't need to. Gina might've been right all along, that it was far-fetched to think the two X's were anything more than random marks made by a flailing man in the throes of death.

She grabbed her cell and fired off a message to Gabe.

*Can you do me a favor? I need to know everyone who bid on the Isidore Bonheur. Is there a way you can find that for me?*

Somewhere in his reams of data from several different machines there was surely *some* way for Gabe to extract the information she needed.

Her phone pinged.

*Yup. Gimme a sec.*

Lacey smiled.

Just then, she heard a noise coming from the back garden. She stood and headed out through the auction room, seeing that the French doors were standing open. It wasn't often that Lacey had much reason to go into the garden. Her plan to use it for outdoor furniture hadn't yet come to fruition, and Gina had taken it over ever since her garden became overrun with lambs. Apparently an allotment was big enough for her to get her gardening fix.

As expected, Lacey discovered Gina clattering around in the greenhouse.

Lacey slid open the door, and a wall of humid air came wafting out at her. She slipped through the gap.

"There you are," she said to Gina's back.

Gina jumped a mile and swirled on the spot. Her hair was pulled off her sweaty face and secured in a bun. Her cheeks were red.

"Lacey. You gave me a fright," she said. She looked very guilty.

"Sorry," Lacey said, narrowing her eyes suspiciously. "I did call for you."

"I had the door closed," Gina said, her carefree tone sounding distinctly forced to Lacey.

"I know. It's like a sauna in here! What are you up to?" She peered past Gina's shoulder, trying to get a look at what she was up to. All she could see was a box of pretty pink bell flowers.

"Just boxing these up," Gina said hurriedly. She pushed a fly away off her face with her gardening-gloved hand, leaving a muddy streak.

"Who are they for?" Lacey asked.

"Just a new client," Gina replied, flippantly.

After landscaping the lawns at the Lodge, Gina had found her gardening services in sudden high demand and had taken on a couple of other interested business owners over the summer—she'd made hanging baskets for a bland office block, had neatened up the outside space of a pub, and had even lent her expertise and green thumb to the local hospital. Lacey wasn't sure where her evasiveness was coming from; if she had a new client that was great news! And she knew she was more than welcome to use the greenhouse for her side business. Lacey had no problem with it at all. In fact, she'd encouraged it, buying her that hydroponic system as a gift and loaning her the use of the greenhouses at the store. It wasn't like Lacey was about to get her hands muddy, after all!

"A new client?" Lacey asked, feeling excited for her friend. "That's great. Well done, Gina. Is it anyone I know?" She was digging now, but it wasn't like Gina to be tight-lipped about *anything*.

"Just a bride," Gina replied, flippantly. "A one-off. Nothing special. She might not even decide to use me."

"I see," Lacey said. She understood now why Gina was playing her cards close to her chest. She just didn't want to get her hopes up over a job that might not come to anything. Lacey knew all too well what it felt like when a good deal slipped through your fingers. Indeed, she had an entire answering machine full of such bitter disappointments. She decided to stop prodding. Gina was quite clearly sensitive about it.

Just then, Chester came trotting in through the open greenhouse door, wagging his tail in a happy greeting. But far from greeting him in return, Gina rushed over and took him by the collar.

"These are poisonous!" she exclaimed. "That's why I had the door closed. We need to keep the pooches on the other side."

She started to tug him toward the door. Chester, clearly perturbed not to have been given as warm a greeting as he expected, put up a bit of resistance, digging his paws in. Which ultimately forced Gina into a game of tug-of-war, which Lacey couldn't help but chuckle over.

*You can't outsmart Chester,* she thought.

While Gina was busy half-dragging Chester out of the greenhouse, Lacey took a closer look at the flowers. They were very pretty, with a dark center, and delicate, papery petals in a gorgeous, deep shade of pink.

She checked the label to see what they were called.

"Kiss-Me-Quick," she said, with a chuckle.

But the laughter died almost as soon as it had started as the word *kiss* began to go round and round in her head. A sudden fear seized Lacey.

The flowers were poisonous. Hugh was poisoned. They were called Kiss-Me-Quick. Hugh had drawn a kiss on the window.

"Silly name, isn't it?" came Gina's voice from behind.

Now it was Lacey's turn to jump. She let go of the tag and swirled on the spot, blinking at Gina as she slid the greenhouse door back into place with a loud click. Through the condensation-streaked windows, Lacey could see Chester pacing back and forth on the other side with agitated movements.

Gina turned to face her and folded her arms. She had an odd look in her eyes, Lacey noted, that she couldn't quite place. A sort of flightiness.

Despite the humidity, a shiver peeled through Lacey. What had Gina done?

"Excuse me, I'd better get back to the store," she mumbled, averting her gaze and charging, head bowed, for the sliding door.

She half expected Gina to stop her from leaving, but her friend just watched her pass with that same look of mournful disappointment.

Chester hurried up to Lacey as she marched along the paving slabs back toward the store, her hand gripped over her mouth to stop herself from crying out as her terrible fear took hold.

She hurried into her small back office. Her mind was racing. She was shaking all over, so flustered she could hardly see straight.

Chester barked at her.

"I know. I know. I'm freaking out. I'm sorry."

She took a long, slow breath in and sighed it out. Then she did it again, and again, until the black stars disappeared from her eyes.

Glancing back over her shoulder anxiously, she logged on to her computer and searched for Kiss-Me-Quick plants.

"Kiss-Me-Quicks contain brunfelsamidine," she murmured under her breath, reading the page she'd found, "a naturally occurring chemical that is highly toxic if ingested by dogs, cats, horses, and even people. If left untreated, clinical symptoms include cough and fever, tremors, diarrhea and vomiting, lethargy and weakness, lack of coordination, seizures, and, in extreme cases, death."

She sank back into her seat, overwhelmed by her thoughts. Was that why Gina had spent so much time out in the greenhouses recently? Had she been growing her own personal supply of poison?

No. It just didn't make sense. It wasn't like Gina to do such a thing. Lacey just couldn't picture it. If Gina had done anything, anything at all, it was surely unintentional. Perhaps she'd just been trying to get her own back on Hugh after he'd threatened them both and attempted to ruin the business? Lacey could quite easily imagine Gina slipping him some diarrhea-inducing substance; it was just the sort of prank she loved and she had an abundance of the stuff on hand so it wouldn't have been hard. Had she just wanted to teach him a lesson? And because he was already sick his body hadn't been able to cope with the poison?

Was that why she'd dismissed Lacey's theory that the X on the window stood for a kiss, and called it far-fetched? Because Lacey had actually gotten way too close to the truth?

Lacey listened to the sound of Gina in the greenhouse. As loath as Lacey was to admit it, her friend was still in the running. She didn't care for the statue. But she did care about the rude man who'd shouted at her and threatened to ruin the business. The real question was, did she care enough to want revenge?

# CHAPTER TWENTY TWO

Lacey sat in her car, mulling it all over. There were no customers to tend to, and hanging around with Gina while she was still a suspect in her mind felt uncomfortable. Instead, Lacey decided to put all her effort into looking at other leads. In fact, she desperately wanted any other avenue to follow so she could strike Gina off her list ASAP.

Gabe had sent her the information about every single person who'd bid on the Isidore Bonheur, and Lacey perused it while Chester napped in the passenger seat beside her.

Mr. Oolong. Sabine Jardin. Dustin Powell. Ciara Oliviera. They'd all dropped out fairly early on, and had secured other wins they'd paid for without quibbling. It seemed like a stretch that they'd be honest on one hand, and a lying, stealing murdering thief on the other.

Then she spotted a French name amongst the list. Jean Bernard Petite. That must be the man she'd nicknamed Monsieur Cheval. He'd left in an angry huff, she recalled, throwing down his bidder's paddle. He'd also been one of the last few in the race for the Isidore Bonheur.

She pondered him. If his wife had thrown a fit over a plate, perhaps she'd done the same when he'd failed to win the statue. Could he have been driven to steal it to shut her up? It was a stretch, but having seen their petty behavior firsthand, Lacey wouldn't put it past them.

She cross-checked Gina's bidders list against her own auctioneer's notes and saw that Jean Bernard Petite had the Exeter Airport Hotel listed as his address. So the couple weren't staying in Wilfordshire, but at least an hour's drive away.

Lacey wondered how they were negotiating the festival situation. They must be driving in each day and spending the whole time in Wilfordshire, attending the various races and events, before heading back in the evening. Since the statue had been stolen during the evening or early hours of the morning, Jean Bernard would had to have been hanging around the Lodge for quite a while to get the chance. Maybe someone there saw him.

It wasn't a huge amount to go on, but it was certainly better than nothing.

She started the car engine, Chester sleepily raising his head at the noise, then headed to the Lodge. She parked around back, beside the bright pink mini, then went straight to the drawing room and up to the bar. If Jean Bernard had been killing time at the Lodge, then he was probably killing it there.

"It's Tony, right?" Lacey said to the mustachioed mixologist behind the drawing room bar.

"Toby," he said, rolling his eyes at the fact she'd gotten his name wrong, like always. "Can I help you, Lacey?"

"I'm looking for someone. Jean Bernard Petite."

"The French guy?" Toby said. "Yeah, he's in here every night with his wife. Weird couple. He seems perpetually stressed, and she cries a lot. They drink whiskey until a taxi picks them up at ten."

"Did you happen to see them the night the statue was stolen?"

Toby twiddled the ends of his moustache thoughtfully. "Yeah. They were laughing at that Ukrainian woman. She came in blind drunk."

Lacey nodded. This was definitely the night of the theft, the one she wanted to know about. "Did they stay long?"

He shook his head. "Nope. Their taxi picked them up at ten, like normal."

Lacey considered it. Oxana got back before the couple left, so there was still a brief window of time for one of them to steal the statue.

"Was there any point where you noticed either of them sitting alone?" she asked.

"Nope. They were together the whole time. Totally co-dependent."

"And when they left, did you notice them holding anything?"

Again, he shook his head. "Something statue-sized? Nah. As far as I remember, they left empty-handed like they do every night. I know it's busy at the moment, but I'm pretty sure I'd notice someone walking off with a statue stuffed under their sweater."

Lacey nodded. This didn't seem to be getting her anywhere. And the mustachioed mixologist might well be confident in his memories of not having seen anyone leave the Lodge with the statue, but the reality was *someone* had.

Lacey headed down the steps of the Lodge, feeling just as baffled as ever. Chester trotted beside her, and the two headed across the parking lot for the Volvo.

On the way, Lacey spotted someone she recognized. Short, plump, and bald, it was Dustin Powell, lucky bidder number one from the auction. Also one of the auction-goers who had cancelled his purchase. She hazarded a wave.

The man spotted her and waved back. "Hello there," he said genially.

"Dustin. How are you?" Lacey asked.

"Happy to be alive," he joked, patting his round tummy. "I've heard not everyone who attended your auction was quite so lucky."

Lacey tensed. It was a weird comment for him to make, and she wasn't sure whether it was just gallows humor.

"Are you staying at the Lodge?" she asked conversationally, jabbing her thumb over her shoulder in the general direction of the grand building.

"I was," he replied. "But I decided to check out early. I don't want to get burglarized. Or … you know … " He mimed slicing a finger across his neck, then chuckled again, too loudly and far too jovially for Lacey's taste.

Her frown deepened. This felt like more than just black humor. It felt like nerves.

Suddenly, Lacey felt suspicious of the portly man. He'd been in the running for the Isidore Bonheur after all, even if he had dropped out early in the race. And Lacey had only really struck him off her suspect list because he'd won other items at the auction and paid for them, and it seemed odd for someone to be honest on the one hand and a crook on the other. But maybe that was exactly what he wanted her to think.

Lacey's mind began racing at a mile a second. Chester whined, looking perturbed as he often did when she frowned too deeply.

"So how come you're back here then?" she asked. "If you checked out early?"

"The menu," he said, tapping his stomach again. "I had to come back for this evening's grouse. No one else in town serves grouse fresh from the field, served a different way every evening!"

Lacey nodded. The shooting club wasn't back to full operation, as far as she was aware, but clearly they were partaking in some activities again.

Dustin licked his lips. "It's roast grouse with bread sauce on Mondays. Roast grouse with braised cabbage, celeriac purée, and sauce Albert on Tuesdays. Mousseline of grouse with pearl barley, savoy cabbage, pancetta, and red wine on Wednesdays." He began counting on his fingers. "Thursday is roast grouse with blackberries and port wine. Friday is pine-scented grouse with cobnuts, haggis, and neeps 'n' tatties. Then Saturday is roast grouse with creamed root vegetables, stuffed cabbage, and elderberries, and Sunday is a spin on the traditional roast—Yorkshire grouse with black pudding and greengages."

Lacey raised her eyebrows. "You've memorized the menu? Are you a food critic or something?"

"A blogger," he said.

"Ah. A food *blogger*."

"No, no," he corrected. "A *grouse* blogger."

Lacey paused. That was an unusual hobby to say the least.

"I'd love to read it," Lacey said, as an idea started formulating in her head.

"You would?" Dustin replied. He looked thrilled. Presumably, not many people shared his interest in grouse. "You can find it at fat man eats dot com."

"Thanks," Lacey said. "I will."

She bade farewell to Dustin and headed back to the car with Chester. Once inside, she retrieved her cell phone and connected to the internet. She typed in the address of Dustin's blog and began to read.

Sure enough, he'd written very long, very detailed, almost blow by blow accounts of every single mouthful of grouse he'd eaten. He'd included the dates and the times—right down to the minute. There was an entry for every single day that week, including the evening that Hugh was murdered. So unless Dustin had a stomach of steel, the likelihood of him lugging his grouse-filled body all the way to Tolleton Green to commit murder—before going home and casually writing up another entry into his blogging odyssey—was rather remote.

Dustin Powell was another dead end.

# Chapter Twenty Three

Evening fell, bringing little respite from the heat of the day. It was the sort of oppressive mugginess that suggested a thunderstorm was coming.

Lacey sat on the picnic bench at the end of her garden, a glass of red wine in one hand, her notes laid out in front of her. She'd gone through her entire list of auction attendees and rewatched the footage that Gabe had sent over. She'd ended up with not a single new clue. Amongst the tourists who'd attended, none of them stood out as particularly dodgy. Of course, when you're dealing with lots of Cayman Island tax haven types, it's not always possible to work out exactly how they made their money, but on the surface it didn't seem as if she'd been harboring any mafiosos.

She stared at her notes. She must have missed something.

She glanced over the hedge at Gina's house. It was in darkness.

Ever since Lacey's discovery of the Kiss-Me-Quicks, coupled with Gina's strange, shifty behavior, Lacey had flitted back and forth on her worry about Gina being the culprit. On one hand, she could see the plausibility of an attempt to get back at a nasty person backfiring on her. But on the other hand, she couldn't imagine Gina staying quiet about it either. If she had "poisoned" Hugh by accident, then Lacey would surely be the first person she turned to, because Gina had no one else, and she had no ability to keep a secret, nor much of a filter. Gina wouldn't lie to her.

But she was hiding something…

Lacey put it out of her mind. She'd drive herself crazy thinking about it. What she really needed was a second pair of eyes.

She retrieved her cell phone from her pocket and scrolled through her contacts. Naomi would be useless. She couldn't sleuth her way out of a paper bag. Her mom would just panic that Lacey had gotten herself into yet another sticky situation. Suzy was too young and inexperienced to offer much support. That left Tom.

Lacey had been avoiding calling him. Ever since she'd met Emmanuel in the patisserie, she'd felt a strange sense of betrayal. It was silly, she knew that much, especially considering how she'd kept Colin a secret from him. But she just couldn't understand why Tom wouldn't tell her something so important, and would just leave her to find out for herself.

Still, they'd have to speak eventually. Why not now?

She hit dial. The phone rang several times. Then it crackled as it was answered on the other side.

As it connected, Lacey could tell immediately from the background noise that Tom was still at the patisserie. He was working himself into an early grave.

"Tom's phone," came the warm Kenyan accent of Emmanuel.

Lacey was thrown. She removed the phone from her ear and checked the caller ID. She'd definitely called Tom's personal number. "Emmanuel? What are you doing answering Tom's cell?"

"I'm Mr. Forrester's assistant now," he replied jovially.

Lacey was so shocked she almost knocked over her wine. How had the charming boy she'd met on the counter earlier gone from till operator to assistant in one working day? And how had Tom, once again, failed to tell her anything about it?

"This is Lacey. Tom's partner. We met earlier."

"I remember," Emmanuel said. Then in a loud, bright voice, he added, "How can I help you, Lacey?"

It was quite obvious he was attempting to get Tom's attention and drop a less than subtle hint.

"I wanted to speak to Tom," Lacey said.

"Let me see if he can talk," Emmanuel said. "He has a last-minute wedding cake testing tomorrow morning, so he's just preparing all the batches."

"Don't worry about it," Lacey interjected. She'd seen the amount of work Tom undertook to prepare all the wedding cake samples for testing and already knew he'd be too busy to focus on her even if he did have the courtesy to try. "I'll catch up with him some other time."

She ended the call before Emmanuel had a chance to say any more, and sat back with a sigh of disappointment.

What was going on with Tom? She felt like she hadn't seen him in a million years. He was busy with work, she knew that, so then why was he still accepting more? It wasn't written in law that he had to take on every bride-to-be that called him to make their wedding cake! And she couldn't help but feel that if he cared for her as much as he said he did, he'd turn down the extra work and prioritize spending time with her. At this stage, it was starting to feel like he was deliberately keeping himself busy. Had Tom gotten cold feet?

Just then, her cell started ringing on the tale, emitting vibrations on the wood. From the other side of the kitchen, Chester barked.

"I've got it," she told him, scooping up her phone. Only then did she see the name flashing at her. *David.* "Great," she muttered. "What does he want?"

Her ex always had a knack for calling her at the most inopportune moment. Right now, when she was questioning her relationship, was knee deep in a murder investigation, and had potentially wasted thousands of pounds on a load of stock she couldn't sell, was of course the perfect time. It was like he had a sixth sense, and could sense from all the way across the ocean that she'd hit her lowest point.

Chester barked again at the continued ringing. She hadn't answered the call yet. Nothing David ever said was good, and she wasn't sure she could handle yet another blow. Then she took the plunge and hit the green button.

"Oh, you are there," David said, sounding surprised. "I was about to leave a voicemail."

"Ta-da," Lacey replied unenthusiastically. "How can I help you, David?"

"I wanted to know if you'd gotten the papers through yet."

"Papers?" Lacey asked.

"The forms. To change your name."

Lacey was at a loss. "I did that when I moved to the UK." She distinctly remembered the process with the deed poll.

"No, I mean for all the leftover accounts and things. Remember? You said there were still some accounts you hadn't changed yet because they all needed different forms, and I said I'd find them for you."

"I thought you were joking," Lacey said.

"Why would I be joking?"

It was a good point. David wasn't exactly known for his sense of humor.

"Are you telling me you researched every old account I've not changed to my maiden name?" Lacey asked, feeling incredulous. It seemed extremely petty. "Why?"

"Because I'm engaged to be married," David stated.

"You are? I thought you split up."

"That was ages ago," David replied, emitting a weary sigh. "We're back together now."

"Sorry," Lacey returned wryly. "I guess I don't commit the comings and goings of your life to my memory anymore."

David huffed. "Stop making this difficult. The point is, she doesn't want you using my name anymore. At all. On anything. I know you changed it legally, but there are still things registered in your old name."

Lacey felt herself tense. "What does it matter? Who cares if my old library card, gym membership, and blood donation card have your name on them? What does she think I'm going to do? Steal her identity?"

David paused for a beat. "Lacey. This is her first marriage. It's important to her that I enter it with a clean slate."

"In that case, are you going to stop having brunch with my mother?" Lacey asked. "I can't imagine the ex-mother-in-law fits into the clean bill she's hoping for."

"Lacey!" David barked. "This is ridiculous. You don't want my name as much as she doesn't want you using it! So just sign the goddamn paperwork!"

"David, the second your paperwork arrives through my letterbox, I'm throwing it on the bonfire!"

The line went dead. Lacey chucked her phone onto the table. It landed with a thud.

She sunk her head into her hands. She was being petulant, she knew that. But right now, this was the last thing she needed. Some petty administrative work she didn't have the time for, nor the mental space to devote to.

The sound of knocking made her start. Lacey stood and walked the length of the corridor. She opened the door to DCI Beth Lewis.

"Detective?" Lacey asked, surprised. Her throat went dry. Was she here to arrest her?

"Please," the woman replied. "We've known each other a while now. We should be on first-name terms."

That was a good sign, Lacey thought. No one would start a conversation with, "We're on first-name terms. Oh by the way, you're under arrest."

"Why are you here?" Lacey asked, reticently.

"I have some news for you."

"The toxicology report?" Lacey asked, her chest lifting with hope. If the report didn't identify brunfelsamidine as the toxic agent, then that meant Gina was off the hook. She desperately wanted it to be the case.

Beth gave her a look. "I know I overstep the boundaries with you sometimes," she said. "But I'm not about to share the results of a toxicology report of a current murder investigation with a civilian, am I?" She gave her head a rueful shake. "I came here to tell you the Isidore Bonheur has been located."

Lacey was stunned. The theft had been solved?

"You did?" she stammered. "Where was it?"

"That's the thing," Beth said. "It was in Hugh Buckingham's house after all. It was very well hidden so didn't turn up in our initial search. But my team was in there today for a final check and found it."

Lacey couldn't believe it. Oxana had been right all along? Hugh was the thief?

But how? How on earth had that sickly man even managed to sneak into the B&B and steal the statue from right under her nose? And not be noticed by anyone?

"Wait," Lacey said, suddenly. "The thief and killer aren't the same person."

"It looks that way," Beth said. Then she shifted awkwardly from one foot to the next. "I should go. I just thought you'd like to now."

"Thank you," Lacey murmured, shutting the door after her.

She turned, resting her back against the door.

Hugh was the thief. Then did that mean Oxana was the killer? Surely it made the most sense. He took the statue off her, so she went in to steal it back. Maybe she'd poisoned him just to render him unconscious, but in his already unwell state the dose killed him. Maybe she'd failed to steal back the statue because it was so well hidden. It had taken the police two searches to find it, after all.

But there was one problem with the Oxana-as-the-perp theory. Lacey had refused to give her his address. So how had Oxana even known where he lived to steal the statue off him in the first place?

Chester nudged his nose against her hand. She petted his silky ears.

"We need to go to the mansion," she said.

Chester looked up at her expectantly.

Maybe she was being arrogant in thinking she'd find something the police had missed, or maybe the fact it had taken them two searches of Hugh's mansion to find the Isidore Bonheur sculpture lent more credibility to the idea that there was something else they'd missed.

She hurried over to the dresser and pulled out a pair of medical gloves. Then she looked back at Chester.

"Let's get snooping!"

Hugh's mansion looked foreboding in the moonlight. The crime scene police tape was gone, just as Lacey had anticipated following her call with Beth earlier that day, meaning it was no longer under guard. She slid her gloves on anyway; even if the police had finished searching the property, that didn't mean she should just leave her fingerprints all over the place.

She stepped up onto the porch. The first thing she noted was how lax Hugh's security had been. No security cameras. No gate. For a rich man, Hugh Buckingham had taken little to no precautions to protect himself from intruders. It was something she'd noticed about England in general, the laissez-faire approach to home security, which was lagging a couple of years behind the U.S. Or a century behind, in Hugh's case.

She tried the door handle, but found it locked. There was a lock box by the door for a spare key, but it was hanging open and the spare had been removed. Removed, or fallen?

Lacey crouched down, parting the leaves of the shrub beneath. There was the key. Strike one against Beth's team; if they'd failed to properly put a key back in a lockbox, what else had they failed at?

Lacey unlocked the door and gave it a push, instantly flashing back to the heavy weight of Hugh slumped against it the last time she was here. She shook the memory off and headed inside.

It was eerily quiet in Hugh's vast hallway. Somewhere in the distance, a clock ticked, but other than that, all was silent. There wasn't even the background hum of electricity. The main supply to the mansion must have already been cut off.

Lacey switched on her flashlight. Chester's eyes glowed in the beam. "You know the drill, boy," she told him.

He scampered off into the darkness, sniffing for clues.

Lacey shined her light at the window behind the succulent, to see if there was any sign of the X marks. But they were long gone. She briefly wondered if they'd ever been there in the first place.

She headed down the corridor, directing her beam at the various pieces of furniture and decorations as she went. Hugh was clearly a very wealthy man. She spotted an Art Nouveau long-necked vase with a squat baluster.

She went into what appeared to be a study and started poking around, going through drawers and stacks of papers, looking for anything that might be a clue.

Chester had his nose to the floorboards, whimpering. Lacey paced over.

"What is it? What have you found?"

She crouched down. Just poking through the gap in the boards was the corner of what looked like an envelope. Lacey took it between her fingertips and pulled. Sure enough, an envelope came out through the gap.

She didn't know whether it had been hidden there, or if it had just fallen between the gaps. It was lightly perfumed with a flowery scent and had pink lipstick on the flap, two indicators that it was a love note. Lacey began to read.

*Hugh*

*My love. You know how much you mean to me. How much I adore you. How I have told you a thousand times over that I will marry you. But I simply cannot and will not sign that blasted prenup. Don't you trust me? It breaks my heart to think you think I'm some gold digger who's only after your money. I am in love with you! What must I do to prove it? How long must I wait before you trust me? Remember how you said I was too young to make such an important commitment? Well, I say you're too old not to! My darling, love knows no boundaries, has no age limits. I wish more than anything in the world that we didn't have to keep our love a secret.*

A sudden noise broke Lacey's concentration. She looked up from the letter and glanced over at Chester. He gave her a head quirk to the side. He'd heard it too.

Lacey discarded the letter on the desktop. There were more immediate and pressing issues to deal with now. She strained to listen. The noise came again, and this time Lacey's breath caught in her lungs. It was coming from downstairs. It sounded distinctly like the sound of the front door being quietly opened.

Someone else was there.

# CHAPTER TWENTY FOUR

Lacey crept to the landing and peered through the banister into the moonlit hallway of Hugh Buckingham's mansion. The door was standing an inch ajar. It swayed slightly back and forth with the gentle breeze. For a brief second, Lacey wondered if maybe she'd just left it open, and the noise she'd heard was the breeze stirring it. But no. She distinctly recalled having closed it carefully behind her, after she'd noticed that the security system was lax. Someone had definitely opened it. But there was no sign of whoever had entered.

Lacey glanced behind her shoulder at Chester, sitting patiently beside the wall. Having him with her always made her feel more calm. She just wished he was able to communicate with her and tell her that everything was okay. Perhaps he could suggest to her that the noise was the cleaner. The house was spotless after all. But even the most loyal of cleaners wouldn't come to a dead man's house in the middle of the night. No. There was an intruder. Lacey was sure of it.

She began to creep down the stairs.

Moonlight streaking through the banisters made shadows dance across her body as she moved. Chester, behind, followed in slow synchronization, somehow immediately able to understand he needed to be quiet. Lacey may well have laughed at the sight of him slowly creeping down the steps with his flank against the wall had it not been for the terror pumping through her.

A sudden noise made her freeze. It was coming from the living room she'd passed on her way up the stairs. It sounded like someone was opening a drawer. Shuffling through the papers inside. Now the drawer was being closed, and another opened.

161

Whoever was in Hugh's house was looking for something.

She should run. She knew that. She should just bolt for the door and race away. Chester would bite anyone who tried to harm her. But Lacey was too curious to flee. She needed to know who was rummaging around in the murdered man's belongings. Because whoever it was might just solve the whole damn case.

Lacey took the final step off the staircase, planting her feet firmly on the marble floor of the hallway. She kept her back to the wall and started inching closer and closer to the open doorway of the living room. She reached the wooden door surround, took a breath, then turned her head to steal a quick glance inside the room. She was braced to see a shadowy figure over by the dresser. She was not expecting to see a face just an inch from her own.

Lacey screamed and staggered back, tripping on Chester. She went flying across the slippery marble floor on her backside. Chester few into a frenzy, barking frantically at the suddenly looming figure. Lacey saw a flash of something metal in the moonlight. A crowbar? A candle holder? Whatever weapon the intruder had on them, they were readying themself to bring it crashing down on her head.

Lacey raised an arm up to protect herself.

"Lacey?" came a voice. A familiar voice.

Lacey froze. She opened her eyes—surprised to discover she'd squeezed them shut in anticipation of the blow—and peered through her arm.

"Oxana?" she exclaimed.

The Ukrainian businesswoman was standing there in her Louboutin stilettos with a brass fire poke held above her head. She was completely still, her mouth open with surprise.

Lacey snapped back to the moment. She scrambled up to her feet. "What are you doing with that thing? You frightened me to death!" she exclaimed.

"I frightened you?" Oxana cried. "YOU frightened ME!"

She lowered the fire poke to her side. Lacey dusted herself down. Her heart was still hammering in her chest. Her coccyx was sore from where she'd fallen on it.

"What the heck are you doing here?" she asked Oxana.

"I'm looking for clues," the woman said brusquely. "The police think I had something to do with Hugh's death. You?"

Lacey eyed Oxana warily. She didn't really trust a word that came out of her mouth. But Oxana didn't need to know that.

"Same," Lacey finally said, with a guarded air.

Oxana folded her arms, looking put out. "So? Did you find anything?" she demanded.

Lacey wasn't going to answer that question, not for a second. But it did remind her of the love letter she'd found up in the study. She'd never gotten a chance to see the signature. All she'd been able to glean from it was that Hugh had a young lover, one who was keen to marry him, but whom he was keeping a secret. That didn't really tell her anything. About half of the men in England were probably in the same situation.

"Nothing yet," Lacey told Oxana. "You?"

The woman shook her head. "Just lots of accounts. Books upon books. They never tell you that being rich can be so boring."

She smiled wryly. It might very well have been the first time Lacey had seen Oxana smile. The only other time had been just before she kissed Hugh.

The kiss. Lacey hadn't given up on it yet. It might still be a clue.

"Hold on," Lacey said, a lightbulb flashing on in her mind. "How did you know where Hugh lived?"

Lacey herself had records in her auctioneering notes. But Oxana shouldn't have been privy to such information and Lacey had refused to give it to her. For her to even be here was incriminating enough, because it proved she'd at some point gone to the effort of seeking out Hugh's address, which was, incidentally, the location of his murder. Oxana had placed herself right in the frame.

"It wasn't hard to find," she replied, shrugging it off. "The internet is a marvel."

Her mention of the internet made Lacey think again about the situation with the failed auction. She'd had a suspicion that Oxana might have done something to cut the connection to make sure she won the Isidore Bonheur. Was that a veiled confession?

"Did the police get in touch with you?" Lacey asked, her mind switching to the stolen statue.

"Not since they questioned me over Hugh's death. Why do you ask?"

"The statue was found."

Oxana's eyes widened with surprise. "My statue? They found my statue? Where was it? Who stole it?"

Lacey wasn't sure how much she should be telling Oxana. But if her behavior tonight was anything to go by, she was something of a blabbermouth. Lacey wouldn't put it past her to talk herself into a confession. She just needed her ego massaged.

"It looks like you were right," Lacey said. "They found the statue here. Hugh must've stolen it when you were passed out drunk."

"I knew it!" Oxana exclaimed, stamping the pointy heel of her stiletto into the marble triumphantly. "Didn't I tell you?"

Lacey nodded, playing along. "What I don't understand, though, is how the murder and the theft connect."

Oxana shrugged. "Maybe they don't. Maybe it's all just a coincidence."

She seemed enthused now she'd learned the police had her statue back. In fact, she was acting like she was vindicated. That now the police knew she'd been right about Hugh stealing her statue, they'd drop their suspicion. But Lacey knew better. She knew how Superintendent Turner ticked. They'd just find a new explanation to fit the scenario. They'd claim Oxana had killed Hugh out of spite, and had left the statue for them to find, knowing it would be returned to her. Come to think of it, that may very well be what had happened. Prickles ran up Lacey's spine at the thought.

"Now what?" Lacey asked, realizing she was standing in a murdered man's hallway with the woman who might very well have killed him.

Oxana slapped her hands as if brushing off the dirt. "I don't know about you, but I'm going back to the Lodge for a glass of champagne and a bubble bath. If the police found my statue, and know I was right about Hugh being the thief, then my work here is done."

She barged past Lacey, heading for the doorway. But before she got there, she halted. "Uh-oh."

Lacey looked up. Lights were flashing through the glass panels either side of the door, illuminating Oxana's face in alternating whites and blues.

The police had arrived.

A moment later Superintendent Karl Turner stepped into the foyer.

"If it isn't my favorite amateur sleuth," he said as his gaze fell to Lacey. "I should've known I'd find you here."

# Chapter Twenty Five

Lacey glared at the reflection of Superintendent Karl Turner in the rearview mirror of the cruiser. She was not impressed with his handling of the situation, but she also knew she didn't have a leg to stand on. Using a key to get into a dead man's house was not an argument that would hold much weight in court, after all.

Superintendent Turner looked in the mirror at her from the passenger seat at the front. "Someone looks sour," he said, a smirk on his lips.

Since he'd asked no question, Lacey said nothing. She noticed the way the driver's eyebrows twitched at the comment, and the subsequent silence. Superintendent Turner's unpopularity amongst the force was not a well-kept secret. None of them seemed to agree with his stuffy, outdated way of doing things, though as his subordinates, they evidently had no recourse to complain.

"You do know you bring this on yourself," Superintendent Turner continued, unperturbed. "Breaking into a crime scene. Waking up the neighbors. Tolleton Green isn't the sort of place where the sight of a beat-up champagne-colored Volvo goes undocumented! Those folks are just itching for the drama."

He guffawed loudly, seemingly very pleased with his put-down. That explained the lack of security, Lacey thought. If everyone's neighbors were as paranoid about an unfamiliar car as Hugh's, the police were probably on call every hour of every day.

Lacey refused to rise to his taunting. But from the caged off section at the back of the car, Chester didn't hold back. He let out a low, long growl, which Lacey couldn't help but smirk at. Sadly she had no such option, so instead, she folded her arms—glad at least that she hadn't been cuffed with those horrible plastic ties—and gazed out the window. She'd have to pick up her car tomorrow. Assuming she wasn't an incarcerated woman tomorrow, that was.

They reached Wilfordshire station, and the driver parked in the lot. Before Superintendent Turner had a chance to even open the passenger door and vacate the vehicle, DCI Lewis's car parked beside him. She'd been following behind with Oxana in the other cruiser. As she pulled up beside her, Lacey noticed just how furious she looked. No wonder Superintendent Turner had insisted on riding with Lacey; DCI Lewis had probably had quite an earful from "Ukraine's wealthiest female CEO (of an Industrial, Plastics or Textile company)."

The driver got out of the car and opened up the hatch to let out Chester. Lacey, stuck because of the safety locks, began to panic. "Where are you taking him?"

"Don't worry. We have a holding pen. He'll be back with you once you're done questioning. It's just for safety reasons." He said it reassuringly enough, so Lacey relaxed.

Superintendent Turner sneered at her. "You know if we were in the U.S we could have shot that dog by now."

"So you keep saying," Lacey replied thinly.

She watched the male detective exit the car and take his time readjusting his pants before languorously allowing her out of the back seat.

"Thank you," Lacey said through her teeth as she emerged into the warm evening.

They followed DCI Lewis and Oxana inside, and Superintendent Turner led them straight through the reception—ignoring the receptionist Lacey was confident was Jacqui—and into the back corridor.

"Lacey, let's have you in questioning room one," he said, pointing at the sign on the door. "Oxana, you can go in two."

Oxana glowered. "That's Ms. Kovalenko to you, you rude little man."

Lacey couldn't help but smile, even if she was still a little suspicious that Oxana was a killer.

Just then, the conjoining door opened and Jacqui the nasally receptionist hurried through. "Detectives. The toxicology report came back. It was cyanide!"

She looked, Lacey dared say, excited by the finding. Superintendent Turner snapped his head to the side and shot her a death glare. Jacqui must've been so excited to pass on the information it hadn't occurred to her that Superintendent Turner had two suspects in tow, to whom she'd just revealed some very important evidence. She slunk back, her cheeks burning red.

But Lacey was overwhelmed with relief. Cyanide. Not brunfelsamidine. Hugh hadn't been killed by Gina's Kiss-Me-Quicks. Her friend was off the hook. But who was back in the picture? Only the three-time winner of Ukraine's wealthiest female CEO of an Industrial, Plastics or Textile company award. Ms. Oxana Kovalenko.

"You've got to listen to me," Lacey said across the table to Superintendent Turner. "Oxana made her money in industrials! She doesn't stop gloating about it. She'd have easy access to cyanide. Whereas I've no idea where to get the stuff."

Superintendent Turner glowered. "I'm going to kill that Jacqui," he muttered, referring to the blabbermouth cop on reception who'd spilled about the cyanide in the first place. He turned his stony gaze to Lacey. "Anyway, that's not what we're here to discuss. We're here because you've been caught breaking and entering."

Lacey immediately shook her head. She was having none of it. "I think you'll find I haven't broken anything. I entered through the front door with the key that was supposed to be in the keypad for the housekeeper, only one of your clever cops didn't shut it properly and it fell on the ground. So the most you can charge me for is trespass."

Superintendent Turner's right eyelid twitched. That was all the evidence Lacey needed to know she had him there. "And you need to stop wasting time on me. There's a whole town out there who wants you to solve this crime, not waste your time on something so trivial."

"If you're so confident about your theory, then explain to me why Oxana returned to the scene of the crime."

"To find the statue Hugh stole off her," Lacey urged. "It was obviously very well hidden if your team couldn't find it during their first sweep of the house."

Superintendent Turner shook his head. "Hugh didn't steal the statue."

"He didn't? How do you know?"

"We pulled prints off it. They didn't match him. Or you, for that matter."

The police had her prints on file, much to Lacey's chagrin. But at least on this one occasion it had been useful.

Lacey was stunned. So Hugh hadn't committed the theft after all? Then who had?

Lacey ran through it all in her mind. It had to be someone who knew the statue was valuable, so an attendee at the auction. And not a remote one, either, since it was highly unlikely someone flew all the way over from Europe to steal a statue. But it also had to be someone who'd witnessed him storming into the antiques store and demanding the statue was his, because they must've known that pinning the theft on him would invalidate his ownership claim.

"What are you thinking?" Superintendent Turner asked.

Clearly, he didn't have this as sewn up as he wanted it to appear, if he was asking Lacey for her opinion.

"During my auction," Lacey said, "the internet cut out at a crucial moment. It meant that Oxana was the winner of the statue, and that Hugh, who was bidding remotely, lost out by just one pound. But because he had a record of having placed a bid, as far as he was concerned, he was the rightful winner. I suspected Oxana had been the one to mess with the connection to make sure she won, which would invalidate her win. But if Hugh stole the statue anyway, it would invalidate *his* claim as well. Meaning the statue was ownerless."

Her mind was whirring now. "The thief had to know where Hugh lived. And there were only two people at that auction with access to that information." Her voice trailed off as a terrible realization sunk in. "Me and..."

"And?" Superintendent Turner asked impatiently. "Who?"

"... Gabe," Lacey said, her chest sinking.

When she'd gone through the list of everyone who'd attended the auction, she'd only looked at the attendees. She'd completely forgot about the three people there who weren't bidding—her, Gina, and Gabe.

The grumpy teenager fit the profile to a tee. He also could have engineered the whole situation with the auction falling through specifically to create the confusion and conditions he needed to steal the statue. He was staying at the Lodge, so he had easy access to Oxana's room. But he couldn't store the statue there, it would be too obvious. He must've gotten Hugh's address from the system, knowing Oxana would immediately blame him, leading to a search of the property, the discovery of the statue, and the invalidation of his ownership.

"Who's Gabe?"

"My tech guy."

"And where would we find him?"

"The Lodge. He's Suzy's neighbor from Tolleton Green. His parents sent him to the Lodge to work for the summer. For character building." Her chest sank with disappointment. Gabe's parents were obviously trying to do the best for him, and he'd thrown it right back in their face.

Superintendent Turner didn't look convinced. But he stood. "I'm putting a lot of faith in you, Lacey. Let's hope you don't let me down."

Lacey stood too. "I think you're forgetting something."

The detective frowned.

"I'm not going anywhere without my dog," Lacey told him firmly.

Turner rolled his eyes. "Fine."

# CHAPTER TWENTY SIX

They entered the Lodge. Emma's eyes widened. Standing beside the local chief gave Lacey more gravitas to be a detective herself, and she wasn't about to pretend otherwise.

"Emma, is it?" she asked the new girl on the desk. "Remember how we talked earlier?"

She nodded slowly. Her eyes were round.

"Is Gabe here?"

The fear in her eyes seemed to subside at the understanding that she wasn't the subject of their scrutiny. "Gabe? What do you want to speak to Gabe for?"

"Can you just go and fetch him?" Lacey asked, avoiding answering the question.

Emma stood with a frown and headed out back. She returned a few moments later with her brother in tow.

"Hey," Gabe mumbled, glancing through his fringe at Lacey first, then Superintendent Turner. His gaze returned to Lacey, now suspicious. "What are you doing here? With the police?"

"Just tying up a loose thread," Lacey said, thinking on her feet. "Superintendent Turner wanted to hear from you directly about what happened to the internet on the day of my auction."

With skeptical eyes, Gabe directed his focus to Superintendent Turner. "There was an interruption on the line. Someone disconnected the internet, so I had to switch to another network."

"You sure someone disconnected it?" Superintendent Turner asked.

Gabe hesitated. "I mean I guess it could've just cut out on its own accord," he mumbled.

Lacey narrowed her eyes. "Could it now?" she said, folding her arms.

When Gabe had called her about the disruption, he'd said in no uncertain terms that human interference had been the culprit. But evidently he'd just been playing on Lacey's ignorance of all things tech related. Now, face to face with the police, he'd been forced to admit there was a more boring possible explanation, that the internet had simply glitched.

"There's no way to know what caused the dropout," he replied defensively. "But you've got to admit the timing is too suspicious to be a coincidence."

Lacey hesitated. Would Gabe really be telling her all this if he'd been the one to do it? In front of a cop as well! Unless he was trying to guide them in the direction of Oxana by suggesting the timing of the dropout was important. Maybe he was as arrogant as his sister, and got a kick out of hiding in plain sight.

"Is there any way to find out who did it?" Lacey asked.

"Not unless you have a security cam in your office. It could only be done by someone either physically powering off your router, or disconnecting the Wi-Fi on your computer."

There were very few people who had access to the office. Her. Gina, whom she'd already discounted. Gabe, who she realized now was just a silly kid getting overexcited, rather than some criminal mastermind.

"Colin!" Lacey gasped.

He'd marched right into her office like he knew exactly where it was. Almost as if he'd been in there before. And he ticked other criteria too: he'd attended the auction, he'd witnessed the altercation between Lacey and Hugh, and he'd been third in line to win the statue. What if he'd dropped out when the bidding had gotten too high, then slipped into the office to interrupt the internet connection, to create the distraction and confusion needed to throw the whole sale into flux?

Colin had been a suspect of hers already. But when he'd come out with all that stuff about only pretending to want the statue so he could see her, she'd just believed him. Had it all been fake? A scheme? Had Colin been playing her all this time, pretending he liked her? Of course it wasn't because he liked her! He had a whole scheme. He was playing the long game. He'd set himself up the perfect cover story in case she figured it out, one that would make her feel so awkward that she wouldn't press it any further.

"Colin who?" Superintendent Turner pressed.

Lacey shook her head. "I don't know his full name. I met him at auction in Weymouth. He's not even local. But he's been following that goddamn statue like a fly! He's been biding his time. I scuppered his plans when we were in Weymouth so he came up with another one." She shook her head. "How was I so stupid?" She'd fallen for the oldest trick in the book. Romantic trickery. Colin must've worked out immediately that she was feeling insecure about her relationship with Tom and used it as an in.

"How are we meant to find this Colin guy then? If you don't know anything about him?"

Just then, Emma spoke up. "He's right there," she said, pointing over Lacey's shoulder.

Sure enough, Colin was walking down the corridor in the direction of the drawing room. Lacey's mouth dropped open with surprise. She turned back to Emma. "He is staying here? The other day you said he wasn't."

Emma looked terrified again, like she was in trouble. "I'm new," she said, defensively. "I made a mistake."

Well, that made Lacey's suspicion even stronger. If Colin had been staying at the Lodge the night Oxana was robbed, then it made it even more likely it was him. Why he didn't just leave town with his contraband was the confusing thing, though. It seemed convoluted to try and engineer this whole situation of invalidating ownership through theft and what-not. It would've been quicker and easier to just run.

Lacey looked at Superintendent Turner. "Shall I talk to him? Try to get him to confess?"

"If you think you can," Karl Turner replied.

With a resolute nod, Lacey followed after him and into the drawing room.

"Colin," she said.

He swirled around, looking surprised to see her. "Lacey? What are you doing here?"

Lacey knew she had to tread carefully here. If she showed her hand too early, Colin would realize she was on to him and clam up. She'd have to ... flirt.

"I wanted to see you," Lacey said.

"How did you know I had a room here?"

Lacey jerked a thumb over her shoulder. "I'm friends with the owner. We're kind of a tight-knit community. Can I get you a drink?" She nodded to the barman.

He smiled, looking pleased. "Sure. Whiskey. Neat."

"Got it."

Lacey's heart was pounding anxiously as the barman poured the drinks and Colin took a seat in the drawing room. She reminded herself last time she was here a man had been shot. She'd survived that. She could survive this.

She took the drinks over to the table where Colin sat expectantly, taking the seat opposite him, nudging it back to get a couple of extra inches of breathing room.

"No Stella tonight?" she asked, trying her best not to sound stiff and awkward.

"She's sleeping," Colin replied. He took the glass and sipped. "Thanks for this. I must say I didn't think I was going to see you again."

"Me neither," Lacey said. "I figured you would've left town by now."

Of course he hadn't, because he hadn't actually managed to get his hands fully on the statue yet. And presumably he wouldn't leave until it had been released from police custody back into either her or Oxana's possession, so he could concoct another scheme to claim ownership.

"I probably should," Colin said. "But I had the room for another night, so thought I'd stay out the end of the festival."

Lacey paused then, reflecting on his last statement. The festival. Surely Colin wouldn't have been able to book a room on short notice. Everywhere had been fully booked weeks in advance, as far as she understood. So either he'd been lucky and managed to get a cancellation, or he'd booked his room well in advance. And since Lacey hadn't even planned her auction until the last minute, how would he have even known the Isidore Bonheur would end up in her auction house?

"You're lucky you managed to get a room," Lacey commented, trying to be covert despite her suspicions. "Suzy told me they were booked up way in advance."

He smiled, and it appeared genuine, as if he wasn't rising to her bait. "I've been to the festival a couple of times in the past. They used to put up stalls, you see, and there was always this one woman from Dorset who'd have a bunch of stuff on offer. I thought it might be worth another shot this year, but she didn't come. Lucky for me, you held your auction, so the trip wasn't a complete bust."

"So you didn't come for me," Lacey said. She was playing it coy and felt guilty for it, but she needed Colin to admit his stories weren't aligning. Either he came here for *her* on a whim as he claimed, or he was always planning on coming here.

"You were the deciding factor," Colin said. He swilled the whiskey in his glass. "I think I might've given the festival a miss this year otherwise. A cancelled hotel room here or there isn't too big a deal, in my opinion."

He had her there. Maybe for someone like Lacey the thought of booking a hotel room only to not use it when your plans changed seemed absurd. But there was another half of the world, the Hugh Buckinghams and Oxanas and, apparently, Colins, who could throw more caution (and money) to the wind.

"You must be disappointed," Lacey said. "You didn't win your statue. And you didn't get the girl."

"Didn't I?" Colin asked.

She looked up from her whiskey glass, feeling her cheeks grow hot.

Colin continued. "Because the girl appears to be sitting with me, sharing a drink on a summer evening. Despite seeing someone."

She coughed awkwardly. She just couldn't do this. Being an undercover agent wasn't her style. "I think we both know you're not really sticking around for me," she said.

"Ah," Colin said. "You figured it out."

Lacey's heart seemed to stop beating. Was he about to confess?

"Figured out what?" she prompted.

Colin's eyes went over her shoulder to the open door of the drawing room. Lacey craned to see where he was looking. It was Emma, the pretty receptionist, who was busy reapplying her lipstick in a handheld mirror.

Lacey turned back, completely confused. "What?"

"Emma. We ... well, we hit it off. What can I say? You'd rejected me, and I was down. And then this lovely young woman started chatting to me. Before I know it, it's two in the morning and we've talked for hours." There was a deep blush in his cheeks.

Lacey was astonished. That was not what she was expecting to hear at all! Any attempt on her part to keep up a ruse failed in one go. "You're hanging around because of Emma?"

Colin looked embarrassed. "I'm a single man. What can I say? I'm sorry. I know I'm a bit of a pickup artist, and I'm sorry you got caught in the crossfire. You don't need to be jealous."

"I'm not jealous," Lacey refuted immediately. "That's not what's going on at all."

Before Lacey fully had a chance to explain herself, Superintendent Turner came marching in. He'd obviously grown impatient of listening to their back and forth.

"Right, you," he said, pointing at Colin. "Can you come to the station with me? We have some questions to ask about a theft in the B&B."

With a stunned expression, Colin looked from the detective to Lacey. "Is he with you?" he asked, sounding hurt. "Did you set this up?"

Lacey didn't know what to say. She let her eyes drop with shame.

"Lacey!" Colin exclaimed, as Superintendent Turner manhandled him out of his seat. "I didn't steal the statue! Search my room. It's not there. I know my story doesn't seem legit, but it is. I came for you, and I stuck around for her."

Lacey said nothing as Colin was led away by the police. But for some reason, she felt like he was being sincere. It had been far-fetched when she'd thought of it, and now she'd have to bend a whole bunch of different things to fit with the theory. Why would he need to scam his way to owning a statue if he was as wealthy as he claimed? The bid he put in at her auction far exceeded the price he knew she'd paid for the statue from the art store in Weymouth. If he'd wanted the statue so much, that would've been the time to get a hold of it! Not later. Not through such convoluted measures.

Lacey realized, too late, that Colin wasn't the thief. She'd led the police right to him and now she had to solve this before an innocent man was sent down for a crime he hadn't committed.

# CHAPTER TWENTY SEVEN

Lacey didn't know what to do. Something was missing. She felt she'd made the wrong call with Colin. Possibly even with Oxana. Nothing was quite adding up.

She went into the hallway and over to the reception desk. Emma was there, peering at the door with an anxious, pained expression. Through the glass, Lacey could see Superintendent Turner leading Colin to the cop car.

"You okay?" Lacey asked Emma.

Emma twisted her lips. "I kinda know that guy who just got arrested."

"Oh?" Lacey asked, feigning ignorance. "When I asked you about him before, you said he was just some guy with a dog."

Emma's big doe eyes went even rounder. "I know," she said, quickly. "That's because the night I spent talking to him was the same night the statue got stolen. I didn't want anyone to blame me for it."

So Colin had been telling the truth, Lacey realized. Emma had just confirmed his alibi. Lacey had gotten it wrong, and now he'd been arrested because of her.

Just then, Suzy entered through the foyer doors and Emma snapped her lips shut as her boss and neighbor floated toward the reception desk like a fairy.

"The cops just arrested someone," she said, pointing over her shoulder. Then she noticed Lacey standing there and a smile suddenly warmed her pixie features. "Lacey! What are you doing here?"

Lacey did a double-take at Emma. The receptionist had averted her eyes, and was now shuffling some pages on her desk, wafting her flowery perfume toward Lacey as she did so.

Lacey frowned. She'd smelled the perfume before…

"Lacey?" Suzy asked again in response to her silence. Worry was now sounding in her voice.

Her mind still trying to place the smell, Lacey looked back at her friend.

"Is it Gabe?" Suzy whispered. "Did he do something?"

Lacey shook her head. "It's not Gabe."

Suzy took her hand and led her to the brown leather couch opposite the reception desk.

"What's going on?" she asked softly, as Chester plonked his head in her lap. "You look perturbed."

Lacey was still racking her brains. The cogs were whirring, and she felt like she was just on the cusp of something… something important.

"It's just all this stuff with Hugh," she said absentmindedly. "I thought I'd worked it out, but now I'm not so sure."

You're playing sleuth again?" Suzy said, sounding frustrated. "I've told you to stop getting so wrapped up in all these investigations. You'll get yourself killed one day."

Lacey, realizing what she'd just said (and more importantly who she'd said it to—the world's gentlest sweetheart) finally came around to the moment. "Trust me, it's not a choice. Superintendent Turner's got it in his head that I'm a bad egg. He suspects me for everything."

Suzy rolled her eyes as she petted Chester. "Look. Run me through what's happened. Maybe I can help."

Lacey was hesitant. Not just because of Suzy's reluctant tone and completely inability to deal with anything squeamish. She didn't want to admit her mistakes. Suspecting Gabe. Colin. Gina. She'd entertained some pretty crazy theories in her quest, and she didn't want her friend to know the reason she'd ended up at the Lodge in the first place. She also didn't want to divulge too much information in a public place, since Emma the receptionist was sitting barely ten foot away.

No sooner had she thought it than Lacey suddenly placed the smell of her perfume. She felt the blood drain from her face as she put two and two together. She'd smelled Emma's perfume on the love note she'd found in Hugh's mansion.

179

At her desk, Emma began touching up her makeup in a hand mirror, applying a shade of shimmering pink lipstick. It was the exact same shade as the lipstick that had been on the flap of the love note.

The love letter. The perfume. The lipstick kiss on the flap.

Emma was the author of the letter. Emma was Hugh's young, disgruntled fiancée...

*Of course!* Lacey thought, as it all fell into place.

*Emma* had access to Oxana's room—she was the receptionist. *Emma* had access to Hugh's house—she was his lover. *Emma* knew the cost of the statue. *Emma* was the thief.

But was she the killer?

Was that what the X on the window had been signifying? That Emma, the woman he kissed, had killed him?

Lacey's mind went a mile a minute, fitting all the pieces together. Unlike her other theories, every single piece slotted perfectly into place. Emma was suspect number one.

But what could Lacey do now? She'd already exhausted the police's patience. There was no way she'd be able to get them to turn around and hear her out after they'd just arrested Colin on her insistence!

She'd have to hatch a plan.

"Earth to Lacey?" Suzy said.

"The statue," Lacey blurted.

"Huh?" Suzy asked, looking confused.

"It's being relinquished tonight," she said, using her projected auctioneer's voice to make sure Emma could definitely hear her.

It worked. Out of the corner of her eye, Lacey saw that her words had elicited the intended response in Emma. She was clearly listening in, her curiosity piqued.

"The police are bringing it back to my store tonight," Lacey added.

Suzy frowned. "Er...okay?"

"I need to go." She stood.

"Lacey?" Suzy asked, standing from the couch. "What's going on? Let me help you."

But Lacey shook her head. "It's fine. I'm fine. I promise. I just have to go. Chester, come on, boy."

She hurried out of the foyer, leaving a baffled-looking Suzy behind her and a curious-looking Emma at the reception desk.

As she trotted down the steps, heading for the parking lot, she grabbed her cell phone from her pocket and dialed a number.

"Beth?" she said when her call was answered. "It's Lacey." She shoved the cell between her ear and shoulder and rummaged for her keys. "I need your help." It was only then that Lacey realized the bright pink mini was quite obviously Emma's. But was it the car of a killer?

She unlocked the door. Into the speaker she added, "I think I've solved this thing."

# CHAPTER TWENTY EIGHT

"Night, Gina," Lacey said, waving from the counter.

Gina hesitated at the threshold of the door, Boudica on her leash beside her. They were both framed by moonlight. Gina looked back over her shoulder. "Are you *sure* you don't need me to stay a little longer? Help you tidy everything up?"

"I promise," Lacey lied.

Gina regarded her cautiously, as if trying to find dishonesty in her micro-expressions, before she finally nodded and left, with Boudica in tow.

The second she was gone, Lacey leapt up, ready to get her plan in motion. She felt bad about keeping it from Gina, but she knew she'd only worry if she actually knew what was planning on doing this evening...

Lacey locked everything up and turned off the main lights, leaving just a single lamp on, emitting a soft, warm, yellow glow. Chester watched her curiously as she set everything up, as if silently questioning her. Which was fair enough, Lacey thought, considering she herself was questioning her plan as well. If she was wrong, and ended up accusing someone innocent of a terrible crime, she'd feel awful. Especially if Oxana really was the perp, and in accusing the wrong person Lacey inadvertently let the guilty party escape scot-free.

But the wheels were in motion, and there was no turning back now.

Lacey headed into the auction room, Chester trotting behind her as she went, ready to protect her should worse come to worst.

She unlocked the back French doors, then immediately jumped out of her skin. There was a shadowy figure standing in the garden. "Emma?"

"Are you still open?" the young receptionist asked politely.

There was no hint of a sinister tone in her voice, nor on her pretty, moonlit face. But Lacey knew looks could be deceiving.

"How can I help you?" Lacey asked. Her own voice, in contrast, sounded stressed.

But Emma didn't seem to notice. She closed the space between them quickly. "I wondered if you could value something for me."

Lacey took a step back, needing a bit of breathing space. Her eyes fell to the bulky object clutched in Emma's sparkly-pink gloved hands. She was holding something wrapped in cloth.

"Of course," Lacey forced, pulling the French door open wider and gesturing her inside.

Emma smiled sweetly as she passed Lacey into the auction room, her flowery perfume scenting the air as she did.

Lacey shuddered. The perfume triggered a visceral memory in Lacey. She'd smelled that delicate floral scent before, on the love letter she'd retrieved from between the floorboards in Hugh's study. She swallowed hard.

They went into the main storeroom, and Emma placed her bundle on the counter. She began to peel back the cloth wrapper and the flowery smell became even more pungent.

Lacey frowned. Had Emma sprayed the cloth with perfume? It seemed like a bizarre thing to do.

Emma stepped back, revealing an antique vase.

Lacey recognized it immediately. It was the Art Nouveau long-necked vase with a squat baluster she'd spotted in Hugh Buckingham's mansion.

Her hands began to shake. This was irrefutable proof that Emma had access to his property. The perfume. The vase. It was strengthening her theory.

"So, what do you think?" Emma asked, sounding completely unfazed. "Is it worth anything?"

Lacey hung back. There was no way she was touching the vase and transferring her fingerprints on to it. That was likely the reason Emma had brought it here in the first place, in an attempt to frame her. If her prints were on something of Hugh's, it would be extremely difficult to argue it away, after all.

But more than the fingerprint issue, some instinct told Lacey not to touch the vase. There was something disconcerting about the fact Emma had sprayed the cloth with perfume. Something that made Lacey even more wary.

Then in a moment of horrible realization, Lacey put it all together. Hugh was killed with cyanide. Cyanide, though mainly odorless, could sometimes give off a smell like burnt almonds ...

Emma was using the perfume to hide the smell of cyanide!

It all made sense. Emma had poisoned the love letter to Hugh, then covered the smell with perfume.

And then it dawned on Lacey that Emma must've put cyanide on the vase too ... She was trying to kill her!

"It's an interesting piece," Lacey began, keeping up the facade. "It's an original Shelley, circa 1890. Looks to be in mint condition. Where did you get it?"

"My fiancé," Emma said dumbly. "He's very wealthy."

Lacey thought back to the contents of the letter. In it, Emma had been lamenting the fact that Hugh wouldn't marry her.

Was she completely deranged? Had she made up a proposal? She was a fantasist. A sociopath!

"Oh, you're engaged," Lacey said, adopting the dreamy tone of a hopeless romantic. It wasn't a role she took to easily, but the prissy Emma might be more at ease if she acted like she cared. "So what's the lucky man's name?"

"H—" Emma began, before clearly realizing her mistake and quickly changing course, "Harry. Harry ... Mann. You wouldn't know him," she added evasively.

"No, I can't say I've ever met a Harry Mann," Lacey replied, wryly.

Emma nudged the vase closer to Lacey, using the index finger of her sparkly pink gloved right hand. "Aren't you going to check this?"

"Are you in a hurry?" Lacey asked innocently.

"No. It's just, it's closing time, isn't it?" Emma said. "I don't want to keep you."

Lacey wasn't about to touch her cyanide vase!

Lacey continued her pretense of examining the vase. "When is the wedding?"

"We haven't set the date."

"Are you going for a lavish ceremony, or something small and intimate?"

"Lavish," Emma said in a floaty voice. "Hugh knows I won't settle for anything less than a big, elaborate event."

She stopped speaking abruptly. By the way her eyes widened with fear, Lacey could tell she'd realized her mistake.

She locked gazes with Lacey and gulped. The cat was well and truly out of the bag now.

"Hugh," Lacey echoed. "Hugh Buckingham. He was your fiancé."

Emma's fear immediately disappeared, replaced by theatrical crying. She'd switched on the waterworks in the way only a true sociopath could.

"I wasn't meant to tell anyone," she said through her crocodile tears.

But Lacey wasn't buying it for a second. Emma had been at work the next night flirting away with Colin! She'd slowly and methodically poisoned her lover because he wanted a prenup? He'd obviously been suspicious of her intentions. And for good reason!

"Emma, give it up," Lacey said. "I know the truth."

"What truth?" Emma wailed, feigning grief.

"You're both from Tolleton Green, you and Hugh. You met there, and wormed your way into his life. You dropped out of college because your only real goal was to marry rich. But Hugh could tell something wasn't right. He was keeping you a secret and he'd only marry you if you signed a prenup."

Emma shook her head as if to refute Lacey's claims. "It wasn't like that. We were deeply in love!"

But Lacey wasn't done. "The only thing you were in love with was his money. He kept you waiting. Gave you his conditions. No marriage until the prenup was signed. But of course you weren't going to marry him with a prenup, because then you wouldn't get any of his money. Why didn't you just walk away? Why did you have to kill him? Was it because

185

your ego was damaged? Or was it because you wanted to remind him his time was running out?"

Emma shook her head, her eyes brimming with tears.

"Did you want him to get sick so you could care for him, so he'd throw caution to the wind and marry you anyway?" Lacey continued. "How long were you poisoning him for? Weeks? Months? You were murdering him by a thousand cuts, weren't you? Inflicting a slow death with cyanide on the perfumed love letters you were sending him."

If Hugh had ingested the poison, he would have died quickly. But through slow, consistent absorption through the skin it had made him sick, giving him a fever and nausea and eventually, respiratory failure. Hugh must have finally worked out what was happening with that last letter and was running out of the house to get help but collapsed at the door. With his last ounce of strength, he scrawled the X's on the window's condensation.

"No!" Emma protested. "That's not what happened at all!"

"And it just wasn't working," Lacey continued, ignoring her pleas. "Despite all your charm, despite all your attempts to convince Hugh his life wasn't lasting forever, he just wouldn't back down on the prenup. Then you realized there was one way you could profit from him after all, even if he didn't make you his wife. You'd seen it before—Hugh buying things from auctions, then the lawyers coming in to add them to his will, a will you were blocked out of, of course. When he told you about my upcoming auction and the Isidore Bonheur statue, you knew the timing was of the essence. You had to make sure he died before he had a chance to get the statue added to his will. Then if you hid it well enough, you could collect it later, once the police had stopped their investigation."

Emma's shoulders shook as she sobbed. "I don't know what you're talking about," she wailed.

"Only problem was," Lacey continued, "Hugh didn't win. Oxana did. But even that didn't faze you. You just had to wait until she passed out drunk, then sneak into her room and steal it. Then you hid it in a place you thought no one would look for it—Hugh's house. But the police found it after all, and your entire plan went belly-up. When you heard me proclaim to Suzy that I had the statue, your greed got the better of you. And you turned up here. With this poisoned vase."

Just like that, Emma's tears ceased immediately. Her act as the grieving partner stopped like someone had pressed a switch. In its place came a look of cold fury.

In a flurry of pink sparkles, Emma snatched up the vase and raised it above her head to throw at Lacey.

But Chester was lying in wait. He came bounding out and leapt up at her, knocking the vase from her hands. The pristinely presented woman went flying to the floor. The gorgeous Shelley vase landed with a crash, cracking clean in half.

"Police!" Beth Lewis cried, emerging from the back auction room where she'd been lying in wait. "You're under arrest!"

# CHAPTER TWENTY NINE

Lacey sat in the waiting room of the Wilfordshire police station, nervously drumming her fingers on her knees. At the sound of the internal door opening, her head darted up.

Oxana waltzed out, her Louboutins thudding on the sparkly linoleum. She took one look at Lacey and grimaced. "Why are you here?"

Lacey stood from the uncomfortable plastic chair. "I just wanted to make sure everything was okay. Did you get the statue back?"

"Yes," Oxana replied, lazily. "I'm the legal owner. I can't wait to get it back to the Ukraine. It will look wonderful in the guest bathroom. Right on the toilet cistern." She flashed Lacey a sly smile, then marched past her and out the door.

Lacey watched her go and sighed. After all that, the gorgeous piece of art was going to be hidden away in the guest bathroom of a Ukrainian tycoon. On the toilet no less!

The internal door squeaked again, and Lacey turned to see Colin striding out into the waiting room.

"Lacey?" he said. "What are you doing here? Isn't it the last day of the festival? I thought you'd be busy at the store."

She gave a little shrug. "I guess I wanted to say goodbye. And apologize. You know. For everything."

"It's been quite the journey, hasn't it?" he said with a rueful chuckle. "Looks like I almost met my match in Emma."

"The player almost got played," Lacey quipped.

"Quite," Colin replied. Then he held out a hand to her. "No hard feelings?"

Lacey shook his hand. "No hard feelings," she confirmed.

Colin gave her a parting nod, then walked past her to the doors. Before he stepped through them, he looked over his shoulder.

"Your partner," he said. "He's a lucky guy."

"Thanks," Lacey replied. "Goodbye, Colin."

He flashed her a grin. "I don't do goodbyes, Lacey. See you later."

She watched him leave, wondering if that really was the last of Colin she'd see, or whether he might just show his face in Wilfordshire again one day.

Lacey returned to the store. It was the last day of the festival. Soon the rich folk would be packing up and heading home and with them the chance of Lacey making back all the money she'd sunk into the auction stock. At least Oxana's payment had cleared for the Isidore Bonheur, but Lacey had still invested a lot in the horse stock she wouldn't get back for at least another year.

The bell went and a short, bald man entered.

"Dustin Powell," he said.

Lacey recognized him immediately. "Lucky bidder number one," she said.

"That's right," he confirmed. "I bought the military riding boots, but then cancelled my order because of ... well, you know ... all that murder stuff."

"I remember," Lacey replied. "How can I help you?"

"I wanted to know if they're still available," Dustin Powell said.

"The boots?" Lacey said. "Yes, they're still available."

"Great. I'll take them."

Lacey stopped herself from acting too happy, though she was ecstatic on the inside.

Amazingly, her store was filled with customers, all looking to buy.

"We heard what you did," one of them said. "You found the killer."

Before the end of the day, Lacey was able to sell all of her horse stock.

She was on a high. With all the extra income, she'd finally be able to hire a new staff member to ease the burden on Gina. Maybe she'd even be able to start holding auction viewing events, like the ones she'd seen at Sawyer & Sons.

Thinking of Sawyer & Sons made Lacey suddenly remember her resolve. She'd promised she would call them about her dad once the festival was over. Well, today was the last day. Everything was drawing to a close. Xavier hadn't been back in touch with any new leads. It was time to bite the bullet.

The pamphlet was still at home in her dresser drawer, but it didn't take long for Lacey to find the Sawyer & Sons website. It was a clunky old one, the sort that needed Gabe's magic programming fingers. She found the number and grabbed the phone.

Her heart was pounding as she dialed the number and listened to the ring tone.

"Sawyer & Sons, this is Jonty speaking, how may I help you today?"

Jonty. The man who had run the auction the day Lacey visited the manor house. The man she was certain was one of the sons.

She cleared her throat. "This might be a very strange question," she explained, "but I'm looking for someone who I believe used to visit your auction house on a regular basis. His name was Frank. And he was . . . "

" . . . .American," Jonty finished for her.

"Yes!" Lacey said, her heart leaping.

"I knew him. You're Lacey, aren't you?"

Hearing her own name shocked her. Her excitement gave way to trepidation. "I am. How did you know that?"

"Because Frank always said you'd find him one day. That one day we'd get a call out of the blue from you asking after him. And that when we did, we were allowed to pass on his message."

Lacey couldn't believe what she was hearing. It was true. Her dad really had been to Sawyer's.

"What message?" she asked, fearing the worst.

"Less a message. More a request. He asked for you to write to him."

"Write to him?" Lacey stammered. "How? I don't know where he is."

"That's why he left his address," Jonty replied.

Lacey's mind began to swirl. Address? Her long-lost father, the man who'd become a ghost to her, had a solid, physical address?

"Can you give it to me?"

"I can," Jonty said. "But I need to remind you he asked for you to write. Not turn up out of the blue."

"I'd send a carrier pigeon if he asked me to," Lacey said. "You have my word."

"One moment. Let me fetch it."

Lacey waited, feeling her hands trembling. She couldn't quite believe this was happening. After all these years, she'd followed all the clues and leads and had finally actually found where her father was.

She heard the phone being picked up again. "Do you have a pen?" Jonty asked.

"Yup," Lacey said, though she was hardly able to hold it in her suddenly sweaty fingers.

"Your father has set up home in Eastwater Bridge, in the Lake District," Jonty explained, as he told her the house number, street name, and postcode.

"The Lake District?" Lace exclaimed. "But that's in the north! I thought my father was in Canterbury."

"He left Canterbury," Jonty told her. "Not that long ago either."

Lacey was stunned as she ended the call.

Her mind was spinning.

Taryn marched in. "Lacey, can you sign my petition? I've decided we need a new Wi-Fi provider for the high street," she said. "The system went down AGAIN and I had to reboot it."

Lacey frowned. "What?" She could hardly comprehend that she was now in possession of her father's address, let alone devote any mental attention to Taryn's Wi-Fi problems.

"The Wi-Fi. You know, the thing that makes the internet happen."

"I know what Wi-Fi is," Lacey replied. "But what do you mean there's a provider for the high street?"

Taryn gave her a look like she was dumb. "Check your options. It's called Wilf_High_Free. All the store owners get it. Don't tell me you've been paying for a separate connection all this time."

Lacey had. But that wasn't important. She checked her settings and saw, indeed, that the Wi-Fi existed. Gabe must have used the local free one to run the auction, rather than her personal one. Then during the auction, the high street Wi-Fi went down, switching them automatically onto Lacey's personal network. All Gabe would've seen at the time was that there was still connectivity—albeit on a different network. But from Lacey's end, the switch occurred during those precious few moments when Hugh was trying to put in a new bid. The internet dropping out right then had been a fluke of timing, and its interruption to her auction hadn't been anything nefarious at all.

The final mystery had been solved.

Lacey felt an overwhelming sense of content that the last piece of the puzzle had finally been put into place. She looked up at Taryn and smiled, gesturing for her to hand over her clipboard and pen.

"Sure," she said, relieved that everything was back to normal. "I'll sign your petition."

# EPILOGUE

After a long and busy day at the store, Lacey locked up and headed into the high street to discover the whole place had been transformed for the end of season party. Gone were all the signs for the tourists, and the window displays of horsey things. Gone, too, were all the summer decorations and bunting. Instead, orange bunting had been hung up, giving the place a distinctly autumnal feel. There were tables lined up on the sidewalks, and children ran around laughing and playing. Lacey smelled barbeque. There was a cotton candy machine. All kinds of fun things.

She'd like to have gone home to get changed, but there was no time. Because at that moment, a flash of pink caught Lacey's eye, and she noticed Gina and her Kiss-Me-Quicks arranged in a lovely display of pink. Curious, Lacey headed in that direction.

As she got closer, she was surprised to see a huge balloon archway, and a banner hung between the telephone poles that read: HAPPY 40TH BIRTHDAY, LACEY.

Lacey gasped. "It's my birthday!" she exclaimed to Chester.

She'd been so caught up in the festival and Hugh's murder, she'd completely forgotten her birthday.

Suddenly, it all made sense. Gina had been shifty because Lacey had caught her growing the Kiss-Me-Quicks which were meant to be a surprise. And there, under the banner and balloon archway, stood all her friends and acquaintances. Nigel. Suzy and Lucia. Ivan. Stephen and Martha. Carol. Jane. Taryn. Beth Lewis. Even Karl Turner!

"Happy birthday, Lacey," they said.

"This is from all of us," Gina said, handing her a certificate.

Still spinning from the shock of the surprise party, Lacey glanced down to see she was holding an official sponsorship pack for a donkey named Alice from the rescue center Gina had mistakenly used the image of for their auction ad. Lacey could tell from the white smudge on Alice's nose that she was, indeed, the exact same donkey.

"Ooh, Gina!" Lacey cried, touched and amused in equal measure. "It's our poster girl!"

"That's the deluxe package, which means you can visit Alice as often as you want," Gina said.

"I love it!" Lacey cried.

Just then, she noticed Emmanuel, Tom's new assistant, standing beside a huge, three-tiered cake. He gave her a cheeky wink. Suddenly, Lacey understood his strange comment when he'd said she looked too young. He must've known Tom was planning this surprise party for her, and was shocked she was turning forty! And the balloon arch! That was why Tom had been on the quiet side road when she'd been in Rosie's cafe with Colin; he'd been going to the balloon store!

Tom stepped toward her with a grin on his face.

"You did all this for me?" Lacey gasped.

All his absences suddenly made perfect sense. He wasn't just busy with the festival—he'd been arranging all of this for her birthday, one she herself had barely thought about.

"Do you like it?" he asked, kissing her.

"I love it!" Lacey exclaimed. "This was what you were doing all that time?"

Tom nodded. "I'm sorry I've not been around enough. I promise to do better."

Lacey shook her head. It felt wrong for Tom to be apologizing after having gone to so much effort to make her fortieth birthday special. And besides, wasn't she the one who really ought to apologize, considering everything that had happened with Colin?

"I need to explain about the other day," Lacey said. "When you saw me in the coffee shop."

Tom's eyebrows drew together.

"It wasn't what it looked like," Lacey said hurriedly. "But I shouldn't have done it. Because of how it looked to others. It's not fair to you."

Tom shook his head and started to chuckle. "Lacey, I hardly even remember what you're talking about. And don't be silly. You can have coffee with whoever you want. I trust you. It wouldn't exactly be fair of me to expect you to sit around twiddling your thumbs on your own while I'm too busy to see you! If people want to gossip about a woman having coffee with a man then that's their problem, not yours. Not ours. I never thought anything untoward was happening."

Lacey felt her shoulders relax. It was a typically Tom response. She'd had no reason to worry at all. Of course her wonderful boyfriend would shrug it off as the insignificance it was.

She flashed him an adoring gaze. "Thank you so much for arranging all of this. It's so sweet. I kind of pushed the whole turning forty thing to the back of my mind. I guess I can't avoid it now though!" She laughed and gestured to the huge banner.

"Actually," Tom said, "you can ignore it a little bit longer, since this party isn't just for your birthday."

"It's not?" she asked, bemused.

Tom shook his head. "Nope."

And to Lacey's astonishment, he bent down on one knee and brought a small black box out of his pocket.

Lacey gasped, her hands going to her mouth. In her peripheral vision she could see her friends gathering around, watching with rapt attention. But her attention was focused like a laser on Tom and the black box as he snapped open the lid to reveal a ring inside. It was an Edwardian-style diamond engagement ring in rose gold.

"Is it ... "

"Antique? Yes, of course," Tom said, laughing.

"Sorry!" Lacey squealed. She was supposed to be quiet right about now, not asking questions about the authenticity of her engagement ring! But you can't take the antique out of the girl. She pressed a finger to her lips. "I'll be quiet now."

Tom flashed her a loving smile. "Lacey," he said, "will you marry me?"

# Now Available!

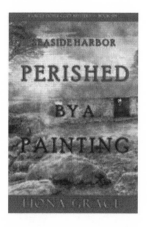

**PERISHED BY A PAINTING**
(A Lacey Doyle Cozy Mystery—Book 6)

"Very entertaining. I highly recommend this book to the permanent library of any reader that appreciates a very well written mystery, with some twists and an intelligent plot. You will not be disappointed. Excellent way to spend a cold weekend!"

—Books and Movie Reviews, Roberto Mattos
(regarding *Murder in the Manor*)

PERISHED BY A PAINTING (A LACEY DOYLE COZY MYSTERY—BOOK 6) is book six in a charming new cozy mystery series which begins with MURDER IN THE MANOR (Book #1), a #1 Bestseller with over 100 five-star reviews—and a free download!

Lacey Doyle, 39 years old and freshly divorced, has made a drastic change: she has walked away from the fast life of New York City and settled down in the quaint English seaside town of Wilfordshire.

Fall has arrived in Wilfordshire, bringing with it Fall festivals of food, charming holidays and refreshing return to simple normalcy. To celebrate their new proposal, Lacey and Tom finally get a romantic countryside trip together, and Lacey is thrilled to stumble upon a rare painting in the most unexpected place—a shack on the side of the road.

But Lacey has no idea how rare and valuable his painting actually is. When she finds out the shocking news, she grapples with whether she should return it—when a shocking twist and a dead body put her right in the middle of a crime that she must, with her beloved dog at her side, solve—or else lose all that she has worked for.

SILENCED BY A SPELL (Book #7), FRAMED BY A FORGERY (Book #8), and CATASTROPHE IN A CLOISTER (Book #9) are also available!

**PERISHED BY A PAINTING**
**(A Lacey Doyle Cozy Mystery—Book 6)**

# ALSO NOW AVAILABLE!
# A NEW SERIES!

**AGED FOR MURDER**
(A Tuscan Vineyard Cozy Mystery—Book 1)

"Very entertaining. I highly recommend this book to the permanent library of any reader that appreciates a very well written mystery, with some twists and an intelligent plot. You will not be disappointed. Excellent way to spend a cold weekend!"

—Books and Movie Reviews, Roberto Mattos
(regarding *Murder in the Manor*)

AGED FOR MURDER (A TUSCAN VINEYARD COZY MYSTERY) is the debut novel in a charming new cozy mystery series by #1 bestselling author Fiona Grace, author of Murder in the Manor (Book #1), a #1 Bestseller with over 100 five-star reviews—and a free download!

When Olivia Glass, 34, concocts an ad for a cheap wine that propels her advertising company to the top, she is ashamed by her own work—yet offered the promotion she's dreamed of. Olivia, at a crossroads, realizes this is not the life she signed up for. Worse, when Olivia discovers her long-time boyfriend, about to propose, has been cheating on her, she realizes it's time for a major life change.

Olivia has always dreamed of moving to Tuscany, living a simple life, and starting her own vineyard.

When her long-time friend messages her about a Tuscan cottage available, Olivia can't help wonder: is it fate?

Hilarious, packed with travel, food, wine, twists and turns, romance and her newfound animal friend—and centering around a baffling small-town murder that Olivia must solve—AGED FOR DEATH is an unputdownable cozy that will keep you laughing late into the night.

Books #2 and #3 in the series—AGED FOR DEATH and AGED FOR MAYHEM—are now also available!

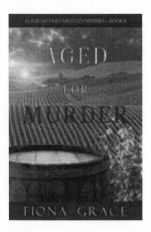

**AGED FOR MURDER**
**(A Tuscan Vineyard Cozy Mystery—Book 1)**